Every bold idea of revenge fled

Gail didn't realize Kyle's purpose in handing the porter the key to his adjoining hotel room—along with a generous tip—until he was leaning against the door that effectively shut out the world.

"Get out of my room!" she ordered.

Amused eyes traveled over her, resting fractionally on the rapid rise and fall of her breasts before moving on to her flushed face. "Come on, Gail," he murmured persuasively, "you're not scared of me and you've certainly been alone in a bedroom with a man before."

"I don't have to take this from you!" she said furiously. "I lived with a married man, but my having his child doesn't give *you* the right to stand in judgment over me."

Books by Alison Fraser

HARLEQUIN PRESENTS
697—PRINCESS
721—THE PRICE OF FREEDOM

These books may be available at your local bookseller.

For a list of all titles currently available,
send your name and address to:

Harlequin Reader Service
P.O. Box 52040, Phoenix, AZ 85072-2040
Canadian address: P.O. Box 2800, Postal Station A,
5170 Yonge St., Willowdale, Ont. M2N 5T5

ALISON FRASER

the price of freedom

Harlequin Books

TORONTO • NEW YORK • LONDON
AMSTERDAM • PARIS • SYDNEY • HAMBURG
STOCKHOLM • ATHENS • TOKYO • MILAN

Harlequin Presents first edition September 1984
ISBN 0-373-10721-8

Original hardcover edition published in 1983
by Mills & Boon Limited

CHAPTER ONE

'Come on, lass, it's a dead one, like its mother,' Calum Mackenzie gruffly informed his niece with the attitude of a man not given to sentimentalising over his beasts. Nature had brought the snow down from the Arctic Circle in high gusts of icy wind, killing some thirty of his flock and roughly a quarter of the spring lambs, and nature was something one couldn't fight.

Gail scarcely registered his impersonal assessment of the small, spindle-legged creature she hugged in the folds of her over-large parka jacket and continued to force warm milk into its mouth. No matter how many they dug out of the high drifts of snow, miraculously kept alive by their mothers' body warmth, it didn't compensate for the depressing sight of a weeks-old baby animal, its body lifeless and rigid with cold.

'Get back to the lorry, girl. I'll look after it now,' Calum ordered evenly.

Gail obeyed, at last recognising the futility of her actions as the milk from the baby's bottle dribbled heedlessly on the snow. Slumped dejectedly in the passenger seat, she realised the foolishness of breaking her heart over a situation she couldn't alter and was accepted by the island crofters as a seasonal inevitability. Nevertheless, she winced at the dull thud of the small weight joining the pile in the back.

Her uncle climbed behind the steering wheel, glanced at her red-chafed cheeks and the slight tremble to her bottom lip, but remained silent on the rought ride back to the farm. The loss hadn't been particularly heavy and Calum Mackenzie, a practical rather than a callous man, counted it in pounds and pence, not in animal life. He

wished the lass wouldn't take on so, but thought none the
less of her for her softness. The day after the snows had let
up, she'd driven down in the wake of the island snow-
plough and uncomplainingly set to the chore with the rest
of them in snow depths that came well over her black
wellingtons, for she was a small girl.

The lorry grated to a halt in the yard and they both
jumped down from the cab. 'You dinna have to do this,
lass,' Calum urged, when she joined him at the tailgate.

'It's OK, Uncle Calley, really,' Gail quickly assured
him, determined to ignore her squeamishness in the face
of her uncle's understanding, and do her share of the
carting of the carcasses into the barn to be stored until
they could be buried later. They worked rapidly and
silently, and Gail almost managed to direct her mind
elsewhere while performing the distasteful task automatically.

'Come in for some tea,' Calum suggested, after fixing
the tarpaulin over the dead sheep and straightening up to
catch the exhaustion momentarily revealed in her earnest
face. Not for the first time, the grizzle-haired crofter
wished he could do something about the sadness reflected
in his niece's wide blue eyes. Island life was hard on all of
them and he himself was resigned to the demands of
scratching a living from the hostile landscape, but he had
wanted more for his sister's child. She was still pretty and
young, but how long before she dried up like her mother,
and the pattern of history became complete? 'We'll put a
tot of whisky into it, eh—for medicinal purposes only,
mind!'

She answered his conspiratorial wink with a smile;
temperance was strong on the island, or at least the
hypocritical lip-service paid to it was. She followed him
out into the yard, but stopped short of the back door.
Granny Mackenzie was hovering over the kitchen sink,
staring out at them.

'I think I'd better be getting home before dark,' Gail justified her rapid change of mind, but they both knew the real reason for her reluctance to enter the farmhouse. It was silly, at twenty-two, to fear the acid tongue of a woman well into her seventies, but to Gail the hunched figure, dressed in habitual black, shoulders draped with a thick woollen shawl, still stirred the childhood imagining that her mother's mother was a witch, and an evil one at that. She pushed the fanciful thought to the back of her mind, but nevertheless veered off towards the Land Rover her uncle had given her on semi-permanent loan. It was very old and therefore too unreliable to be much use in the day-to-day working of the land.

She switched on the ignition; the engine coughed once, spluttered and then died on her. She clicked the switch several times, trying to half threaten, half enchant it into life with, 'Is this the way to treat someone who saved you from the scrap heap? It's been one awful day and I'm tired and wet, and the next time I turn your key, I expect you to start. Is that understood?'

But if Land Rovers really had ears, this one was obviously deaf, she mused, as it refused to do more than whine mournfully. Her uncle appeared at the side window and she fervently hoped he hadn't heard her pleading to the old hunk of rusting metal. Recently she had found herself carrying on two-sided conversations inside her head and, even worse, talking out loud to another distinct self. Like old Annie MacIver, she thought ruefully, who was said by her neighbours to be touched because of her incessant chatter to a husband dead thirty years or more; personally Gail sympathised with Annie's safety valve against the loneliness of living alone.

'The damp weather's got to the engine,' her uncle pronounced his verdict on the battered motor. 'I'll get Rory to fix it and I'll run you up.'

Before she could accept or reject his offer, Granny

Mackenzie's bent frame appeared on the step of the back door, and she called to her son in Gaelic, the musical language sounding harsh and discordant on her lips.

Suddenly being alone didn't seem such a bad situation to Gail, not if one compared it to living fifty years in the same house as her granny, who looked on any form of entertainment as a sin against God and had unmercifully bullied her husband and children all her life. A lift was certainly tempting, saving her the mile uphill journey to her crofter's cottage, but it was more than likely her uncle's kindness would be rewarded by a spiteful haranguing from her granny on his return. For the sake of peace, she passed up the offer.

Gail could dimly see the road ahead through the freezing fog and the sky was darkening ominously, the clouds threatening more snow. She set a fast walking pace, but her wellingtons failed to properly grip the treacherous surface, a layer of ice fast forming on the flattened snow. Her stomach lurched each time she slid and almost lost her footing, and she was relieved to recognise the rise beyond which lay her home.

The sound of an advancing motor abruptly cut through the eerie quiet and sent her scuttling off the narrow single track road and scrambling up the high bank of churned snow. From this vantage point she watched unseen the progress of a sleek blue sports car, so alien to this environment, as it emerged out of the swathes of white fog and slithered up the icy incline. When it went into a deep skid, she instinctively shut her eyes, held her breath and mentally muttered a prayer for the safety of the driver, expecting any moment the sickening sound of metal smashing against stone, for the car was careering towards the dyke on the opposite side of the road.

When she braved herself to look once more, she saw in disbelief the tail-lights of the vehicle disappearing over the brow of the hill. Relief gave way to annoyance for the scare she had been given. Doubtlessly an early tourist who didn't know the road petered out two miles past her home at a disused slate quarry, and she considered it sheer idiocy to be out in these weather conditions, unless strictly necessary.

When her heart ceased racing, she slithered down to the road, the seat of her trousers now as wet as the rest of her. The first snowflake touched her nose and she jerked up her fur-rimmed hood. Shoving her hands, chilled even through woollen mittens, deep into her jacket pockets, she continued on.

By the time she reached the top, her breath was coming on short pants, freezing in the sub-zero temperature, and her toes were numb. All she wanted to do was set a match to the fire, flop down in an armchair and call an end to this frustrating day. In this mood she groaned inwardly at the sight of the same blue car carelessly drawn up on the verge outside her garden wall. That was all she needed—to have to furnish directions to some stupid tourist who hadn't the wits to carry a road map, she thought, and instantly chided herself for her lack of charity.

Slowly she rounded the car's streamlined body and cautiously peered in through the passenger window. The car was unoccupied, but she lingered, her attention riveted by the car's interior. Her eyes rounded with childlike fascination at the plush, deep blue carpeting, the cream leather upholstery and the walnut dashboard that resembled the control panel of a light aircraft. Multiple dials and switches made her wonder irreverently if a pilot's licence was mandatory for this absurdly ostentatious motor car.

Hearing a noise behind her she hastily jumped back, embarrassed at giving way to curiosity about the luxurious vehicle, and promptly tumbled into soft wet snow. Gail cursed her clumsiness and impatiently brushing off the snow, scanned the road and garden, deserted save for herself.

The garden gate swung violently in the rising wind, and after she had whipped off her mittens and secured it with the makeshift wire hook, her fingers were aching and her temper in no way improved. Skirting the stone building, her footsteps muffled by the snow on the pathway, she halted at the sight of a man, bent almost double in his effort to peer into the kitchen window of the low-ceilinged cottage.

'We normally shut gates in the country.' Her voice, despite the lilting, sing-song accent of the north-west coast of Scotland, was as chilled as the rest of her.

If she had hoped to disconcert the stranger with her noiseless approach and accusing tone, she was disappointed as he straightened and slowly turned, apparently unconcerned at being caught trespassing. Instead cold grey eyes travelled over Gail, sharply assessing and eventually returning to rest on what little could be seen of her face through fur and bright wavy hair. And it was she who was rocked by reverberating shock waves at the first glimpse of his familiar features—the sculptured contours of the boldly masculine face, the long, straight nose, and that square jawline—like a ghost from a past she had considered buried beneath a painfully-acquired outer shell.

'You're not going to faint, are you?' He registered her dizzy swaying with a marked degree of detachment.

The deep, unfamiliar voice brought back a measure of balance. As his head came back in focus, she saw hair that was perceptibly darker and cheekbones more pronounced and angular, and she realised that the fading light had been playing tricks on her, distorting a resemblance into something infinitely more sinister.

'No.' Her voice grew stronger as she partially recovered from her fright. 'No, I'm not. I'm sorry, but for an instant you reminded me of someone . . . someone I used to know a long time ago.'

The stranger seemed to accept this and continued, 'By your reaction I would say it was somebody you didn't particularly wish to meet again.'

Ignoring his dry comment, Gail brushed past him, and with awkward, shaking fingers tried to fit the key into the heavy lock.

'Is that your car?' she threw over her shoulder.

'Yes, it is,' he confirmed, drawing closer and pitching his voice higher above the wind.

Her rather unnecessary question had been an attempt to disguise her lingering nervousness, but his short response served to highlight it, making her feel foolish. Irritation crept into her tone when she asked, 'Are you lost?'

'No, I don't think so,' he responded firmly, aware of but indifferent to her impatience to get rid of him. 'I'm looking for Gail Mackenzie.'

Gail wheeled round and stared hard for a second before her eyes veered away again. 'Why?'

'Business,' he offered succinctly.

'Tax?' She matched his verbal shorthand, flushing guiltily as she recalled an official form, half read and stuffed out of sight in the drawer of her bedside cabinet. He met her question with an impassive expression which she took as confirmation. 'I meant to fill it in—honestly I did. But I . . .' she faltered on the verge of making the ridiculous excuse, used by the older generation islanders, that she couldn't read English, and added lamely, 'I forgot. If it's about the work on the farm, I don't receive wages, just some fuel and food as payment, and I didn't think you could tax food. You can't, can you?'

If anything, the movement of his mouth at her anxious appeal revealed the barest hint of amusement. It was unexpected—a taxman with a sense of humour—but then he didn't look much like her image of a taxman.

'If we could go in,' he suggested smoothly, somehow implying a lack of basic courtesy on her part. 'I don't exactly find your climate pleasant and you look rather cold yourself.' His eyes slid over her shivering body. Astute, he interpreted her stubborn stance on the step leading to the back door and his assurance was tinged with mockery as he added, 'I'm not interested in your valuables.'

With his polished, refined accent, he was clearly telling her that anything she might consider of value, would most definitely be beneath his notice and a quick resentment flared inside her. She abruptly pushed open the kitchen door, but he followed closely behind her, not allowing her time to give way to the temptation of slamming the door in his supercilious face.

His gaze wandered round the room, which was devoid of all but the most rudimentary essentials. Gail, fighting to keep a rein on her temper, almost sensed him cataloguing it in some compartment of his mind—the heavy, coal-fired cooking stove that had not been lit for days; the linoleum, curled with damp; the cracked stone sink with its anti-quated pump for cold water.

Before he could draw out one of the wooden chairs which she had grave doubts would hold his weight, she hurriedly lit a candle and led the way through to the tiny, windowless hall at the front of the cottage. Resting the candle in its saucer on top of the coat-stand, she shrugged out of her green jacket and pulled off her boots. She picked up the candle once more and indicated with a cursory nod that he could use one of the vacant hooks for his coat. He ignored the gesture, his cool, appraising eyes fixed on her face and hair, illuminated by the flickering candlelight and he said abstractedly, 'I *thought* it was red, but it was difficult to see under the hood.'

The quietly-spoken remark seemed totally out of context, and it startled her. What did it matter to this man what colour her hair was? Nevertheless she found herself contradicting him, 'It's not red.'

'Red-gold,' he conceded, still with an air of satisfaction.

Gail, unnerved by his unwavering scrutiny, regretted her habit of taking people on trust. She should at least have asked to see some identification, or something. It was too late now; she had already let him into her home. Her doubts chased across her face and were answered with a mild smile that aggravated more than it reassured.

The hall seemed smaller than ever, and she moved quickly into the living room and was immediately conscious, even in the half light, of the poverty of her furnishings. She curbed the instinct to start collecting up the scattered papers and books thrown carelessly round the room, as though she was ashamed of her modest home.

Instead she crouched down beside the hearth. The fire refused to catch light, partly because snow had fallen through the chimney on to the papers, but mainly because the matches kept dropping from her frozen fingers. And all the time she sensed him hovering nearby, watching her, and it made her increasingly incompetent. If Her Majesty's Government gave its tax inspectors courses on how to intimidate their victims, this man must have been one of its star pupils!

As yet another match fell on to the grate, he coolly announced, 'I'll do that, if you want to change out of those wet clothes.'

It sounded like an order, although phrased as a suggestion, and Gail obstinately resumed her inept efforts to light the paper base, until she was seized with a fit of coughing, a symptom of the chest infection that had plagued her throughout the winter months.

Without warning, she was pulled firmly upright by strong, steadying hands than spanned her thin arms and, using an unnecessary force, she immediately wrested herself from his hold, unable to control a violent shudder. Of distaste or fear, she wasn't sure which.

'What's wrong with you, woman?' he rapped out, losing some of his composure in his surprise at her response to his help.

He might well ask, Gail thought; she couldn't understand her own overreaction to his proximity. 'I have a cold,' she mumbled with total inconsequence, giving a light cough as if to confirm it. It sounded absurd.

'That's why you jumped away from me as though I was the one with a contagious disease?' His voice was tinged with disbelief.

'I don't like being touched,' she said over-vehemently.

'Well, considering your aversion to it,' he drawled mockingly, 'you'd better get out of those wet clothes before you end up being touched by a doctor.' Gail opened her mouth to dispute his right to order her about in her own home, but, acutely conscious of the growing exasperation revealed by his deep frown, she thought better of it; as she stamped through to the bedroom, she tried to well a rising fury at his high-handedness. Common sense told her that she could not afford to alienate the man. 'Not in your financial state,' she reproved herself out loud, while she rapidly changed into another pair of faded denims and blue Shetland wool polo-neck. Perhaps she owed taxes from when she had last worked, or maybe they suspected her of undeclared earnings from her work on the farm. Surely she could clear herself of that; her lips quirked with amusement at the image of the imposing stranger being confronted by her granny who would, with little prompting, hold forth at great, scathing length on the subject of her idle, ungrateful granddaughter who didn't deserve any payment. Granny Mackenzie certainly hadn't shown much restraint the first and only time Uncle Calum had suggested it. Instinct told her that would be a scene well worth watching.

Perched on the bed, Gail tried to bring order to her straggling locks, but the comb proved worse than useless, for she seldom bothered with her hair now, apart from keeping it clean. She threw the comb back on the rickety dressing table and spoke sharply to her reflection. 'You're a mess! Do you know that, Miss Gail Mackenzie?' Her ears picked up the sound of her 'guest' moving around the room on the other side of the wall, and she thought regretfully that the cottage deserved the same shameful description. She'd been letting the place go lately, but tomorrow she'd . . .

Conscious once more of the stranger pacing in the next room, she brought immediate practicalities to the fore. She rifled through the drawer and was relieved to find the offending form, albeit excessively crumpled. As she smoothed it out, her eyes ranged quickly over the words but making little sense of the contents. Stilling her impatience, she took it line by line, but was not comforted when she at last understood the official jargon enclosed. The word rebate leapt out at her. Tax inspectors didn't make the difficult journey out to the Western Isles simply because one of their customers failed to claim money *from* them. Control was called for, and watchfulness. That was what he had been doing, she realised, allowing her to babble on confusedly while giving away nothing. She delayed long enough in the hall to catch her breath and clear her throat.

The fire was lit and the room now illuminated by the two oil lamps, and she felt unreasonably cross at his efficiency. He had taken off the camel-hair topcoat and she saw a tall, broad-shouldered man of about thirty-five, dressed in a smart grey lounge suit and spotlessly white linen shirt; it was rare to see anyone dressed so formally, save for island weddings, and of course funerals, and never in such perfectly fitting clothes, underlining the muscular breadth of his chest, and the tapering, narrow hips. In profile, with some relaxation in his expression, she was again affected by his similarity to another. She wanted him gone.

'Why are you here?' she asked bluntly, dispensing with formalities and the resolution to play his game, hoping to catch him off his guard, as he had not noticed her return.

'Are we alone?' he said on turning, and at the ill-concealed alarm in her expressive, wide eyes, added, 'I thought I heard you talking to someone.'

Blushing furiously, Gail fixed on a point above his head. 'I was . . . The wind. Sometimes it makes you hear voices.'

'How disturbing!'

His comment brought Gail's eyes flying suspiciously back to his face, and again there was that slight quirking of his well-shaped mouth. She was mortified by the distinct impression that he saw right through her hastily improvised explanation, and she stood dumb and momentarily tongue-tied.

'May I sit down?' he enquired politely.

Was the wretched man always in control of every situation? He indicated he was waiting for her to seat herself before good manners allowed him to take a chair, and with ill grace she threw herself into a threadbare armchair that flanked the fireplace.

Gail listened to the crackling of the logs on the fire and concentrated her attention on the flames licking up the flue. The silence between them grew and grew, and with it the tension inside her, until she blurted out, 'You're not a taxman, are you?'

'I never said I was,' he returned smoothly.

'You let me . . .'

'Draw your own conclusions,' he admitted unabashedly. 'Otherwise we might still have been on the doorstep with you doing your Flora Macdonald impression of repelling the enemy.'

'I've been up since first light this morning and I'm

tired. Gail's my cousin, but she's away at the moment—on holiday—so if you don't mind I want to be alone,' she declared bluntly, forgetting in her anger that her earlier statements contradicted this barefaced lie. 'If you give me your address . . .'

'I called in at your uncle's farm on my way up here. It would probably save some time if we dispense with the amateur play-acting, Miss Mackenzie,' he returned icily, all mildness gone. The time for appraisal was over. His next words were said with an unmistakable calculation, for the maximum of impact. 'My name is Kyle Saunderson. I'm Barry's brother.'

'Barry!' she echoed. Memories flooded back, unsought, overwhelming in their intensity. Barry's handsome face—like this man's in feature, but transformed by laughter, and a refusal to take anything seriously.

Her single exclamation was deliberately misinterpreted. 'Surely you remember, Miss Mackenzie. Barry *Saunderson?*' All aloof detachment had been dropped: his sarcasm was heavy and undiluted by any trace of humour.

But it scarcely touched Gail as time rolled back. Herself at seventeen, scared of life and yet eager to embrace it, sure in her mind that the world had more to offer than one small Scottish island. And she had been right, there had been more, much more—Barry, and love . . . and eventually heartbreak. She tried to shut out the images of the past, sweet and painful, threatening to engulf her in their whirling, devastating tide.

'Yes, I remember him. I was very sorry to read about his death.' She strove for the right note of polite but impersonal condolence.

Apparently she achieved her objective, because he said, with the same sharp edge to his voice, 'You're harder, Miss Mackenzie, than even I expected.'

'Barry and I were friends, but it was a long time ago,' she justified her apparent lack of emotion that verged on indifference, the nails biting into her palms telling a different story.

'Friends!' he rasped. 'Well, I've heard it called a lot of things, but . . .'

'I don't know what you're trying to imply,' she interceded sharply, her eyes shifting from the flames to meet his head-on. There was no way she was going to expose her feelings to this man's merciless view. It had been over a long time ago, had even happened to a different person.

His steel-grey eyes flickered over her figure in the tight, patched jeans and shrunken jersey, that outlined her extreme slimness but also drew attention to the distinct womanly curves.

'I'm sure that in four years the men in your life have been too numerous to count, Miss Mackenzie, but I would have thought an affair that lasted for several months was not beyond your powers to recall.' The hostility, kept initially below his polished surface, was now blatant, in the narrowed eyes and cruel line of his mouth.

'Affair'—how she hated the word, with all its sordid connotations! Was he stabbing in the dark, armed with some vague rumour and hoping to find a vulnerable spot? Brazen it out, an inner voice urged. If she really were innocent, she would be shouting him down. Belatedly but convincingly she did just that, but with cool haughtiness.

'Mr Saunderson, you appear to be suffering from some delusion concerning my relationship with your brother. Unfortunately I have no witnesses to your crazy, slanderous accusations, but that wouldn't prevent me from taking action, legal action, if you persist in making them!' She had touched a nerve, beating a tattoo at one black eyebrow, and his knuckles showed white against the dark brown cloth of the settee. The tables were turned.

His struggle for control was visible, an urge to violence transmitted by his very rigidity, and it took all Gail's courage to stare unflinchingly back. The reply to her threat, when it eventually came, was measured and quietly spoken, but threaded with a raw, tearing cruelty.

'Have you also conveniently forgotten your bastard child?'

He couldn't have inflicted more pain than if he had struck out physically. Gail wanted to cry out, to shout, 'Haven't I suffered enough yet? Haven't I paid for my weakness?' But this man was her tormenter, not her judge, and any such appeal would be wasted.

'Do you need any places and dates to jog your poor memory, Miss Mackenzie?' he continued on the offensive. 'Edinburgh General, July the . . .'

'Is that why you've come?' she cut in to the reminder that was wholly unnecessary.

'Partly.' He was back to watching, anticipating her breakdown, confident of having regained the upper hand.

A sense of self-preservation ordered her to fight back; she could not allow him to rake over dead ashes.

'My bastard, as you so explicitly described him, was not Barry's,' she announced with a firmness that wiped the superior, scorn-filled expression from Kyle Saunderson's face. 'And he was adopted as a baby, so he isn't mine any more either.' Never was, she added silently. Only once she had seen him—for a few precious seconds through a haze of agony as she had given him life. She pushed the image away from her.

Kyle Saunderson looked . . . stunned, his black head jerked back on the armchair, much more affected by her lie than she had expected, and she took advantage of it. Rising on legs that were not quite steady, Gail forced herself to play out the charade. 'So you can go home and tell his widow that whichever gossipmonger told her that fantastic story was lying!'

When he followed her actions and rose to his feet, she was filled with relief, believing him ready to leave, and therefore having no defence as his strong brown hands clamped down on her shoulders, pressing relentlessly against bone.

'Don't shrink from me,' he commanded harshly at her automatic flinching from his touch. Gail stood her ground, but he did not remove his hold and she wondered if he was deriving pleasure from the pain his tight grip was inflicting. 'Barry and his wife were divorced over three years ago and she no longer has any interest in his affairs. Does that make a difference to your story?'

'No. Why should it?' Had part of her really grown as callous as she sounded?

'Where do you think the boy is?'

Confused by his sharp question, she muttered vaguely, 'With a couple in Edinburgh, I think.'

'Don't you know? Don't you bloody well care?' His fingers bit viciously into her flesh.

'My uncle in Edinburgh arranged it,' she explained, tilting her head in defiance, 'and no, I don't bloody well care!' She stared steadily up at him, still under the pressure of his punishing hands and showing no softness to his searching eyes.

Just one word he breathed, 'Whore!'

'Tramp, harlot, slut!' she hurled back at him, out of a searing rage that held no trace of shame. 'You see, Mr Saunderson, I know all the right words for a woman like me.' They had been mumbled behind her back on this sternly religious island, and once, by her cousin, to her face; they had kept her away from her home for the best part of three years.

His eyes ranged freely over the top of her body and she felt as though she had just been stripped naked for his inspection. They moved back to the soft waves that framed her oval face, with its fresh, faultless complexion, a small nose that had the merest hint of a tilt, and a beautifully shaped mouth that needed no lipstick to draw attention to its fullness. Her eyes, vivid blue and sparkingly alive with her anger, were shadowed by long, curling lashes, shades darker than her red-golden hair. Considered individually her features were not classically beautiful, but their combination was arresting, lending her an air of Peter Pan youthfulness that was piquant and charming.

Only her looks seemed to find no favour with Kyle Saunderson, as he pronounced cuttingly. 'I'm surprised my irresponsible, womanising brother wanted to bed someone like you—even allowing for the adequate packaging!'

'How could I have mistaken you for Barry—even for a second? While he was light, you are darkness.' Gail ran on, contradicting her earlier denials. 'Were you jealous of him, of his popularity, the fact that everybody liked him better?' She couldn't imagine anyone liking this man, far less loving him. 'Barry—he was warm and loving and alive. But you—you're dead to any real human feeling, I wish it was you that was . . .' She didn't finish it, profoundly shocked by the dreadful thing she had been about to say.

But she didn't need to. A muscle quivered at his jawline as he savagely dragged her closer until their bodies touched, and she became aware of the hardness of his thighs against her slightness, suffusing her flesh with a disturbing sensation that had to be fear.

'I could prove here and now that I'm not dead inside!'

Recognising the nature of his threat, Gail panicked, struggling frantically to free herself, her small fists pushing futilely at the wall of his chest. Kyle Saunderson laughed mockingly at her efforts, so ineffective in the face of his dominant strength, and easily trapping her flailing arms behind her back with one hand, he grabbed a handful of hair and yanked her head back. Slowly, tauntingly, he lowered his mouth until it was a bare inch from hers. Gail's response was desperate as she twisted her head away, her eyes watering with the agony of hair almost pulled from its roots.

As abruptly as he had grabbed her, he pushed her forcibly back into her armchair. 'I'm not that hard up,' he said incisively, his breathing not quite even. 'And I'm not the weak, self-deluding fool my brother was.'

Her cry of outrage was cut off by a racking, enervating cough, and she covered her face with hands that shook.

'Here.' A scrupulously white handkerchief was shoved roughly under her nose. 'Have you any whisky or brandy?' She shook her head without looking up. 'Can I make you something hot to drink?' There was no kindness in the question.

'No electricity,' she mumbled.

'Do you wear a hair shirt as well?' he taunted, and with brusque impatience, when her cough became aggravated, he muttered, 'I have some brandy in the car.'

His retreating footsteps sounded loud and angry on the wooden floor and she heard the front door swung wide on its rusty hinges. Sure she was alone, Gail wiped the tears she had been hiding and leaned back on the armchair, inhaling a deep, steadying breath. Her cough, convenient but not contrived, subsided to an irritating tickle in the back of her throat.

How much more could she stand of this emotional battering? Not much. She shut her eyes tight against the tears forming. She could cry later, when he was gone. But not now. Kyle Saunderson had ruptured the even, unemotional rhythm of her life, opened the floodgates to sweet and bitter memories alike, and was souring them for her with his dirty mind. She had been a married man's mistress, and she did not use her ignorance to make excuses for what she herself considered a sin. But she intuitively knew that Kyle Saunderson was no saint either.

'So why am I letting *him* punish me?' she asked aloud,

and when she couldn't find a satisfactory answer, a fierce anger broke through the misery and sent her flying to the door.

CHAPTER TWO

With a reckless urgency, Gail forced home the stiff bolt and caught her fingers in her clumsy haste. She sucked the sting from their grazed tips and leaned heavily on the oak frame, although the door had withstood the harsh island elements for over a hundred years and she was confident that no man, however, strong, muscular and angry, would be able to batter his way through. Let him try! she thought with an uncharacteristic maliciousness after she gingerly touched her own bruised shoulderblade.

Her heartbeat refused to slow, and she was annoyed with her own fear that didn't lessen as the seconds and then the minutes ticked by. How long did it take to fetch something from the car and walk back the fifteen or so yards of pathway?

Nerves stretched to breaking point, she crept back to the living room, twitched back the cotton curtain and saw . . . nothing. No impression of movement in the darkness, as though her silent prayer had been answered and Kyle Saunderson really had been spirited away by the night. Except she no longer believed in 'things that went bump in the night' (or in this case didn't), and over six feet of flesh and bone did not disappear into thin air!

From a standing start her brain raced furiously on, thoughts crowding in on each other. He'd heard her shut the front door; he'd gone round to the back of the cottage; and the kitchen door was . . .

Running, stumbling blindly through the hallway to the kitchen, desperate to shoot the bolt on the back entrance, Gail was stopped midflight, like a rabbit mesmerised by the bright headlights of a car.

Kyle Saunderson misinterpreted the mixture of guilt, embarrassment and shock that made her eyes enormous in her startled face, and quickly swerved the torchlight down to the basket on the table.

'I'm sorry if I frightened you. You needed more logs for the fire,' he explained to the breathless figure he had momentarily trapped in the beam of his torch.

'I . . . I . . .' she stammered incoherently.

'It would make even me jittery—the wind creaking every floorboard and rattling the window panes. You shouldn't live up here on your own. Still, you're probably safer than in the centre of a big city.'

The soft, conversational tone was intended to talk her gently, gradually down from the fright he had imagined in her fever-bright eyes. He had gone round the back to pick up firewood; he wasn't aware of her rash, idiotic attempt to bar him from her home; and somewhere out in the cool night air he had lost that aggressive threatening anger.

'Here, take the torch, and lead the way through,' he instructed quietly.

The hand that felt for hers was cold, but its effect was electric, and her nerveless fingers refused to grip the torch but sent it clattering to the floor. The noise helped her to gather some of her scattered wits and she mumbled throatily, 'I'm sorry.'

Aware of her fine, nervous trembling, his hand dropped away.

'Let's go back to the warmth,' he murmured, scooping up the torch and guiding her through to the living room.

Gail allowed him to think her quivering response was to the cold and, seated once more in front of the fire, she obediently swallowed some of the raw spirit from the flask he drew out of his jacket pocket. The brandy was reviving and raising her head, she automatically smiled her gratitude. His answering smile was warm and attractive, but she looked away immediately, feeling the ground shifting under her feet.

'Drink some more if you want,' he offered softly. 'I'll fetch the wood.'

Gail gripped the flask hard, staring sightlessly down at the initials carved on its silver face and desperately trying to come to terms with his personality change. Kyle Saunderson had left her as Mr Hyde and come back as Dr Jeykll, and she wasn't sure which was the real man, or strangely which one was the more disturbing. Perhaps she could backtrack to the beginning, tell him her side . . .

The shower of sparks sent up by the crashing of a fresh log on the fire broke into her speculation and snapped her head up, as the sole of his shoe kicked the wood viciously back against the chimney wall.

'Wh-what's wrong?' she stuttered, badly startled by the hot fury sparking from his savage expression as he glared down at her, which was an alarming world apart from the compassion he had shown but moments before.

'What's wrong? Such innocence! I commend you on your ability to act, Miss Mackenzie.' His words had the effect of chipped ice, chilling yet stinging. 'But I don't think even your gale force winds are capable of bolting a door from the inside. It's a pity you weren't faster on your feet, isn't it? No wonder you looked ready to keel over when you saw me, and how you must have wanted to laugh when I thought you were frightened by the unexpected noises coming from the kitchen and played chivalrous male to your damsel in distress!'

And she was going to confide in this evil-minded brute! She jerked angrily to her feet. 'I have every right to bolt my door against any passing . . . vagrant who invades my privacy and . . . and makes threats towards me because of something which happened a long time ago . . . and is none of his damn business!' Her voice rose with her temper.

'I rarely *make* threats, Miss Mackenzie,' he ground out, now with a discernible effort to control his own reborn anger, 'and never to a puny five-foot specimen of a sex I have invariably found to be weaker, mentally as well as physically.'

'And *I* am never intimidated by an arrogant, six-foot-odd specimen of a sex I have invariably found to be full of bluster and hot air,' Gail parodied recklessly. Hands clenched by her side, she returned his menacing stare, and unbelievably she sensed some of his anger ebb away, or at least cool till his face was a rigid, passionless mask.

Eventually he broke the tense, building silence with, 'You really aren't frightened of me, are you?'

'No, I'm not,' she flashed back. 'Why should I be?'

'I'm more than a head taller than you, almost twice as heavy and infinitely stronger, but you're not frightened of me,' he laboured each point, as though he was addressing a backward child. 'If you don't mind me saying so, Miss Mackenzie, you are either incredibly brave or remarkably stupid. I suspect the letter.'

Gail considered herself neither brave nor stupid, only now was not the time to back down, to show herself a coward to a man who had no weakness.

'Get out of my house or I'll . . .'

'Or you'll what, Miss Mackenzie?' he challenged, hearing the fight draining from her voice.

Or she'd what? she silently asked herself the same question. Scream loudly, when her nearest neighbour was a mile away and her cry would be lost in the howling wind? The last throes of temper that had burned hot and high called him a muscle-bound bully, but common sense won out.

'Please, Mr Saunderson, it's very late and I . . . it's time you left.' Her forced meekness was abandoned the second she caught the twitching of his lips that reflected an enjoyment of her reluctant humility.

'Surely you're not worrying about your reputation?' he commented dryly. 'And I have no designs on your virtue or lack of it.' His eyes flicked disparagingly over her ragged clothing, but went still for a long moment on the small, upturned face that held no consciousness of its beauty, trying to make sense of that impression of innocence in her soft, vulnerable mouth. His dismissive gesture was directed at himself, as he dragged his eyes away and drawled, 'I like my women with style and breeding, not all eyes and baby dimples. How old were you when you had the baby—fifteen?'

'Eighteen,' she snapped.

'So you must be twenty-two now.' He fixed back on her mutinous expression. 'You don't look more than a teenager. Amazing to think that you're the mother, biologically speaking, of a four-year-old child,' he said with a slow deliberation.

Gail, winced, unable to disguise the wounding accuracy of his barb, and sank back on her armchair. The personal remarks about her immorality she could just about take, but not his reminders about the baby; she didn't need them, for not the passing of four years, or forty, would allow her to forget, even if she wanted to. Daily she nursed the pain, without being aware of it. Her eyes opened once more at the cutting edge of his voice.

'I thought you didn't care,' he threw her earlier assertion back at her.

'I don't,' she declared tautly, 'I just don't want to talk about it.'

'Well, I'm afraid you're going to have to. I haven't come all this way just to tell you what I think of you.' He had regained much of his icy calm as he returned to the two-seater sofa and stretched his long, powerful legs in front of him. 'As you probably know, as well as being a journalist, my brother owned a half share in the family business, left to us by our father.' Gail shrugged her indifference; she had not known Barry's financial status, had never been remotely interested in it. Kyle Saunderson's face reflected a hard disbelief as he continued, 'From the generous cheques he sent you, you must have deduced that he was a wealthy man.'

So she was a gold-digger along with her other, seemingly endless collection of vices! Marching over to the desk in the corner by the window, she brought the flap down with a sharp bang and rummaged through the pile of loose papers until she discovered what she was looking for. She scattered the uncashed cheques down on the empty sofa beside him.

'Every penny is there, Mr Saunderson. Just over fifteen thousand in all, as you no doubt have already calculated. I don't want, never did want a part of his conscience money. Take it and go!'

His black eyebrows lifted fractionally, but the hardness was still there. 'A grand gesture. Let's see how you react when the sum isn't so paltry.'

He referred to fifteen thousand pounds as if it was petty cash, when it would have kept an island family clothed and fed for five years! Gail sat down again, asking suspiciously, 'What do you mean?'

'I thought that might get your interest,' he responded cynically. 'My brother left you his shares of the family business. Or more precisely you and your *love* child, whom he foolishly imagined to be his as well.'

Each cold utterance accused her of scheming and conniving; it was ridiculous and unfair—she hadn't seen Barry in over four years.

'I . . . I don't understand,' she expressed her incredulity, 'Why should he do that?'

'Maybe you were the love of his life, after all,' he bit out, his heavy sarcasm telling her exactly how he viewed such a notion. 'Not just one of the many tramps he got himself involved with.'

'He was your *brother*!' she protested against his vilification of a dead man, no longer able to defend himself.

'I hardly think you're in a position to be critical in the matter of family loyalties.' Pitilessly he alluded to the baby he assumed she had abandoned with total ruthlessness. But she didn't owe him any explanations, didn't care what he thought of her, and she remained silent. 'And Barry was as careless in death as he was in life. While he provided for you and his supposed bastard, he failed to leave anything to his legitimate son. Can you imagine how *he* feels?'

He was charging her with the other boy's unhappiness, but his tone doubted she had an ounce of compassion with which to respond. 'I don't want any of it,' she cried unhesitatingly. What use was money to her? 'He can have it!'

'I think you should know what you're so magnanimously turning down, Miss Mackenzie. It's not a half share in a corner shop.'

The incongruity of this dark intense man who had a surfeit of pride and haughtiness, serving behind a grocery counter, almost brought a smile to her lips, but she controlled the impulse, as she countered adamantly, 'I don't care if it's a . . . a shipping line!'

'It's a very profitable engineering works, worth about three million at a conservative estimate.' His eyes said, 'Let's see you give up your claim to that'.

This time she did laugh; the whole thing was ludicrous—from near-pauper to millionairess because of some foolish romantic whim or misplaced sense of obligation! She was sympathetic to this man's anger, but he had said too much, far too much for her to show it. Her response was flippant to hide her confusion. 'I assume there's a country manor as well.'

'Yes, there is. Do I detect a waning of that touching if

wholly unconvincing altruism?' Kyle sneered, his mouth forming a thin, tight line.

Gail wanted to confound him. 'I can just visualise it now—tea on the lawn, china cups and silver service, of course, the butler hovering, anticipating my every need. Well, thanks, but no thanks. Long English summers and gracious living aren't my scene.'

'I didn't imagine they were, Miss Mackenzie. Your natural setting, I imagine, is a rather dimly-lit nightclub where the air is thick with cigarette smoke and alcohol fumes.'

Gail was lost by his latest line of attack. 'If you haven't noticed,' she drawled with an incisive sarcasm that matched his own, 'the island isn't exactly crawling with night life.'

'But you haven't always lived here, have you?' he pointed out knowingly.

The light dawned. 'Have you had me invesitgated?'

'I hired an agency to track you down, yes.'

For the first time he was on the defensive. The vision of him sifting through some file, impersonal in tone but nevertheless detailing her life, albeit inaccurately, fired her with indignation. 'Next time you need some *snooping* done,' she laboured the condemnatory description, 'I suggest you find another private detective. In the meantime, send me the necessary papers and I'll sign all property over to Barry's oth . . . son.' In anger she was careless. The trouble with lying was, having started, it seemed to snowball until you were forced to weigh everything before speaking.

She was consoled by his apparent lack of awareness of her near slip of the tongue as he tapped his cigarette on its gold case. It came as no surprise to see him using an expensive, initialised lighter, also undoubtedly gold; he would be intolerant of anything but the best, in whatever context.

'You'll have to come back to England with me,' he announced eventually, his lips betraying his distaste, Gail was sure, at the idea of suffering her company. He went on to explain, 'I'm not risking you having a change of heart the minute I've left, and there's no way I intend returning to this desolate uncivilised hole.'

'You recognise I have one—a heart, that is,' she replied with renewed flippancy, disregarding his absurd declaration, which was tantamount to an order and inwardly seething at his derogatory dismissal of her homeland.

'Anatomically speaking, you must have,' he said in a clipped, precise tone.

'Do you have such a low opinion of all women, or am I a special case?' she asked with mock sweetness, not really wishing to know the answer to her question, but merely seeking release for the aggression that was building up inside her.

He was back to watching her, gauging her reaction as he responded, with perfect seriousness, 'There are two places where a woman is useful—in the kitchen and in a man's bed.'

Gail fervently hoped she wasn't blushing at the crude emphasis he gave to the word 'bed'. Not even the average Scots male, traditionally encouraged in chauvinism, approached his bigotry. She wondered fleetingly what had soured him to her sex, and then dismissed the personal thought, concluding that he was born ignorant. Rather than an outright refusal, she resorted to lying once more. 'I'm due to start work in a week or two and I haven't the time to spare to go back with you, simply to sign some papers.'

Kyle inhaled deeply, then casually flicked ash at her waste basket, crammed full of a day's worth of rubbish. 'Where is this "job"?' His tone insinuated a doubt in her ability, far less inclination, to do what he would consider proper work; only his probably misreading it as a ploy to gain his sympathy stopped her from showing him her calloused hands.

'It's in London,' she offered grudgingly.

'When do you leave?' he fired back.

Gail had the strangest conviction that he knew she was lying, but her hesitation was fractional. 'In the next few days. I have to find somewhere to live.' Surely a permissible bending of the truth? After all, Peter Mason, for whom she had worked in Edinburgh, had written several months ago with an open-ended invitation to sing in his new club.

'Singing?' he enquired blandly. 'Or do you provide a more comprehensive service?'

'None of your damn business!' Let him think what he liked. To her, the implied insult was ridiculous: she was sitting opposite him, dressed in what she freely admitted to be the shabbiest of clothing and yet he visualised her as the sort of woman who hung around shady nightclubs and gave a pretence of singing. 'Anyway, you can see it's impossible for me to accompany you, so . . .'

'We live an hour by train from the centre of London,' he dispensed briskly with her objections.

Gail felt she had just dug a pit and then jumped into it herself; the smug curving of his mouth was not lost on her. Her voice rose. 'I don't want to go anywhere with you! Is that clear enough for you?'

'What you do or do not want to do, Miss Mackenzie, is completely irrelevant. When do we leave?'

Counting rapidly to ten, she drew in a deep breath. 'We seem to be having a problem with semantics. Tell me, Mr Kyle Saunderson, has no one ever said the word "no" to you before?'

His face was set in a mask of studied gravity as he responded to her blatant sarcasm with, 'Not often, Miss Mackenzie. And never twice.'

'And how do you propose to *persuade* me to agree? Put me in the boot of your car and drive off?' she suggested mockingly, her blue eyes alive with challenge.

'I shall not leave your cottage until you do so,' he stated implacably.

He wasn't, couldn't be serious in his threat. One look at his hard, unrelenting expression, giving the impression that his overly handsome face had been chiselled out of stone, told her he was.

'So what?' she replied, with a shrug of assumed unconcern. 'I can't see you staying for long. It's not the sort of accommodation you're used to, is it?'

'One night should suffice,' he remarked dryly. 'Or perhaps you really are impervious to what your neighbours and family would think of having a total stranger staying the night?'

Kyle Saunderson had been astute enough to realise that for all her apparent immorality, she would most definitely mind his staying, but not clever enough to see the fallacy of his plan.

'And how are they supposed to know about my supposedly wanton behaviour? My nearest neighbour is more than a mile away,' she countered triumphantly.

His response was a smile that never quite reached his eyes, but nevertheless transformed the harsh, angular features until once more she was strongly, devastatingly reminded of Barry. 'Simple, Miss Mackenzie,' he retorted, his mouth twisting cruelly, 'I would make it my business to tell them.'

Alarmed blue eyes clashed with granite-grey ones that told her more clearly than words that he had every intention of carrying out the threat, would probably derive some satisfaction in doing so. It was not his reputation that was at stake. Not hers either, she argued logically—that had been lost a long time ago. But for the past year, the islanders had been thawing towards her, and despite their narrow, unforgiving temperament, they were her people. She was forced to capitulate.

Reading the conclusion in her eyes, Kyle instructed curtly, 'Be ready tomorrow. At nine sharp.' He rose to his feet in one fluid movement, and she followed his action, instantly uncomfortable with his height advantage over her. 'I'll leave you to get a good night's sleep. Among other characteristics of the typical female that I despise is unpunctuality.'

'Oh, I'll be up well before nine.' His glance was keen, having noted the absence of defeat in her assurance, and Gail covered her rashness with, 'I'll have to pack my clothes.'

'If that's an example,' he declared witheringly, indicating her jeans and pullover, 'I shouldn't waste too much time.'

Gail's fingers itched to slap his arrogant, autocratic face. He answered her savage look with one of equal ferocity, their eyes duelling for an endless moment, his daring her to slap his proud, fine-boned face and promising swift retribution, and hers claiming her lack of fear despite the fact he towered over her slightness.

Remarkably, Kyle Saunderson was the first to break the deadlock, his expression undergoing a confusing transition from white-hot anger to some deep, unfathomable emotion, and then back to his former impersonalness as he cut the tension between them with, 'I'd better go or I'll be locked out.'

Gail didn't bother asking him where he was staying—there was only one hotel on the island, and that was a rather grand title for it. Abruptly he turned on his heel, as though he could no longer bear the sight of her tilted face blazing with youthful defiance, and she slammed the door the moment he crossed the threshold, sending home the bolt with unnecessary force.

Long after he had gone, Gail sat in front of the fire, clutching Barry's cheques in her hand. For the last two years she had lived in, if not for, the present, on her island sanctuary. The future she rarely contemplated; the past was constantly with her in the lonely ache for a part of her she had given away, but it was kept at bay by hard, physical toil and the exhaustion that resulted. Her routine had been simple; up at dawn, work most days till dusk and then crawl into her bed, too tired to think or feel or dream.

But Kyle Saunderson had violated that sanctuary and destroyed her impassive acceptance of this joyless, monotonous existence. Two months ago she had cried for Barry and the tears had washed away much of the bitterness, enabling her at last to forgive the man she had loved so much. This time the tears did not come to release her from the agonised longing for what might have been; instead the memories crowded back to torment her . . .

The leavetaking had been short and for once she was grateful to Granny Mackenzie for her waspish tongue. Ever since Peter Mason's astounding offer of a chance to sing in his folk club, her cousin Rory had been pressurising her to stay, with his solemn, hurt glances and his disdainful remarks about life beyond the shores of their safe island home. She refrained from commenting that Rory's one trip to Glasgow did not qualify him as an expert on the outside world, for she felt guilty about her defection. They were best friends as well as cousins, shielding each other from the harshness of their grandmother.

When she had been on the verge of weakening, abandoning the adventure that was both daunting and thrilling, her grandmother had hardened her resolve with dire warnings about the sinfulness of Edinburgh and her sly insinuations that her despised granddaughter would no doubt be in her natural element in the 'dirt and muck' of the city.

'Bad blood,' her granny mumbled her favourite insult

like a witch's curse, glaring at Gail dressed in her Sunday best of tartan skirt, trim navy jacket and beret cap, set at a jaunty angle.

'Goodbye, Granny. Take care of yourself.' The young girl smiled stiffly through her hurt, biting back the sudden urge to boldly announce her own theory on the origin of any 'bad blood' that ran in her veins.

Rory took her down to meet the ferry in the lorry, and in the last hurried moments of farewell, placed a clumsy kiss on her trembling lips, with more ardour than expertise, hinting at something she had barely suspected.

The boat tugged slowly out of the tiny harbour and her stomach was gripped by an awful wrenching sensation, not alleviated by Rory, standing motionless and grim, refusing to answer her frantic waving.

Before she reached the mainland she was assailed by a loneliness that would have sent her back on the next boat, if there had been another that day. As it was, she had little choice but to carry on to Inverness, where she spent the night with her mother's cousin.

The next morning, with fresh courage, she boarded the Royal Scot at the very last minute. Guitar case in one hand and suitcase in the other, she trailed up the train, from compartment to compartment, hoping to find one that was not crammed full with holidaymakers. After the length of a carriage packed with public schoolboys released for the summer and discussing in high, childish voices cricket scores and rugby tactics and future holidays with boisterous relish, she was almost despairing when the miracle of six empty seats occurred.

She took up a corner seat, thanking some lucky star, and opened up her novel. Within minutes the unfamiliar rocking of the express and a residual tiredness from the first leg of the journey had her fast asleep.

'Ticket, please.'

The voice intruded into her dream. Her eyes flickered

sleepily open to be caught and held by a handsome, boyish face stilling opposite her, studying her with unabashed interest.

'Ticket,' the ticket collector repeated in a monotone.

Gail's disorientated gaze wavered from the smiling stranger in the seat directly opposite up to the railway inspector. Colouring at his barely-concealed impatience, she frisked her jacket pockets for the offending ticket and offered it with mute apology in her eyes.

'This is second class, miss.'

'I bought it in Inverness at the station this morning. I asked for a single to Edinburgh,' she explained huskily, but the collector's attitude did not soften. The unconscious appeal of her slightly-parted lips did not, however, go unanswered.

'You must have been given the wrong ticket,' the young man facing took her part, rising to his feet. 'I'll deal with this.'

Gail did not know how her champion did deal with it, because he ushered the inspector out into the corridor, and after a whispered discussion, returned calmly to his seat. Gail blushed once more, only this time it was caused by his wide smile creasing the corners of his warm, laughing eyes.

'Thank you. What did I do wrong?' Gail enquired shyly.

A pleasant laugh teased her confusion. 'Have you never been on a train before?'

'Yes, of course I have,' she defended huffily, mentally crossing her fingers.

'From the Isles?'

'Yes,' she confirmed his guess.

'Well, for future reference, you may travel first or second class. The first class compartments are more luxurious and usually quieter, and sometimes you meet some very interesting people in them,' he announced with a deliberate charm that was effective in spite, or perhaps because, of its being much-practised.

'And my ticket was second class,' she deduced, appalled by the gaffe she had made.

He laughed again and then bantered with a liberal flattery, 'You are real, aren't you? Not some mountain spirit, fresh with morning dew and sunshine trapped in her hair—a figment of my imagination.'

'A very fertile imagination,' she commented dryly, determined to put him in his place, for the conversation was moving too fast for her liking.

'I hope so,' he responded without offence. 'I'm a journalist.'

'Oh, you'd need it, then—an imagination, I mean,' Gail remarked quite seriously, and was cross when he threw back his head and laughed uninhibitedly.

'Converting dull true facts into a more "readable" account,' he suggested.

'I didn't mean that,' she protested.

His mouth straightened at her note of distress and he tilted his head to one side, eyes running over the face of a shy teenager with her quaint beret, perched sprightly on long, gold-bright hair. 'No, you didn't, did you?'

Was he mocking her again, only with a sudden intentness in his tone? And what had happened to her natural reticence with strangers and acquaintances alike? Gail rose abruptly and turned to get her suitcase down from the rack.

'What are you doing?'

'I'll have to go to another compartment.'

'Because of me?' he challenged mildly.

'Of course not!' she exclaimed over-vehemently. 'I haven't the right ticket.'

He turned her gently round, pressed something into her palm and set her down again. 'You have now.'

No wonder the ticket inspector had passed on—and she

had thought he had been trusting her to move of her own accord. Fumbling into her handbag, she brought out her purse and pulled out some of her precious pound notes.

'How much do I owe you?'

'How about your company for the rest of the journey as payment?' he countered smoothly.

Rory had been right: she wasn't ready to be let out on her own, not if she got herself involved with strange men, even if they did have laughing eyes and the most handsome face she had ever seen.

'I can't . . . I mean, you're a stranger, and . . .'

'. . . Your mother told you not to accept sweets or train tickets from older men,' he finished for her, not put out by the suspicion on her open face. 'Well, so you can ease your mind about talking to strange men. My name is Bartholomew Michael Maclennan Saunderson, and I'm partly Scottish, but mostly very English, as you've probably guessed,' he mocked his mouthful of a name and his drawling, upper class accent, and then, appreciably lower. 'And you're most definitely the best thing that has happened to me since I arrived in your beautiful but grim country.'

Gail sat dumb, not knowing how to respond to the careless compliment, not sure if she should.

'If I didn't have a conscience, then surely the panic in your lovely blue eyes would give me one,' he continued lyrically.

'I didn't think you were . . .' she halted, too embarrassed to complete her denial.

'Oh, but I was,' he replied enigmatically . . .

But it hadn't mattered a damn about their good intentions, because that first meeting had sparked off a sequence of events that had brought pleasure, and pain, and in the end, disillusionment with life itself.

Even now, years on and armed with a greater knowledge of life, Gail wondered if things could have been any different. She had been naïve and trusting, not for one moment considering the possibility that lighthearted, loving Barry was committed elsewhere. She had been wide open to his persuasions that they were so close that a piece of paper binding them would be a mere formality, that their loving made it right and good, because she had been scared of boring him with her rigid island morality, when, by every look and gesture, Barry was expressing how much he adored her.

Could it have been any different? From the instant she had opened her eyes to catch him staring at her, she had been his for the taking. And still, in a way, was bound to him, but it was difficult to conjure up his light, good-looking face without the intrusion of another's, robbing her of the tenderness for Barry that had lingered despite everything, and causing a bitter anger that made her feel startlingly alive with its intensity.

She stood up decisively and fluttered the crumpled cheques down on to the last glimmering lights of the fire. No, she wouldn't go with the elder, ruthless Saunderson. She could torment herself with her own guilt, but some instinctive sense of survival told her to avoid any more of his brutal punishment.

CHAPTER THREE

Gail opened her eyes at six-thirty, despite the fact that it was still pitch dark outside. There never had been any problem in rising in the cottage, because one was woken by the hurting cold that crept up the limbs as the body lost the protection of deep sleep.

Normally she rose quickly, for it was no luxury to lie, getting colder by the second, but this morning it took several minutes to recover from the bout of coughing that racked and weakened her tired body. That was all she needed—the return of her chest problems. It was tempting to blame someone else for her condition, but she knew her stubborn refusal to immediately go and strip off her damp clothing was the cause.

When the coughing subsided to a raw, grating in the back of her throat, she wrapped herself in the top blanket and padded barefoot to the jug and bowl on the dresser. Breaking the thin layer of ice that had formed and dipping her face in the bitingly cold water, she saw the action through Kyle Saunderson's eyes—all so unnecessarily primitive. Hair shirt mentality indeed!

Gail was still coughing intermittently when she finished tugging on rough work cords, and another ragged jersey, and she longed for a hot drink to soothe her burning throat; the effort, however, required to stoke the coal-fired stove and boil a pan of water was too daunting. Perhaps she would be given something when she collected the Land Rover; she prayed that Rory had taken it into his head to fix it.

Scribbling a hasty, far-from-polite note, which she stuck half in, half out of the letter flap in the front door, she

42

started downhill. At least very little snow had fallen in the night and the road had remained relatively clear. The light from the heavy torch was dim, the batteries nearly dead, and she wished she hadn't bothered with it. She had more than enough to cope with in her tartan holdall, stuffed with clothing for the few days she planned to stay away from the cottage. She didn't really need the light to see; she had taken this road down to the bottom of the hill for ten school years, and she knew every twist and turn.

It seemed a time for looking back, but she had little nostalgia for her childhood. The illegitimate daughter of an island girl, she had from her earliest recollections been treated as such—something for the women to whisper over with pious relish and regard with scorn or pity, as the mood took them. It must have been worse for her mother, who had rarely left the environs of their home, but as a child she had only felt the neglect. Even when she had been very small, her mother had never accompanied her; it had been an initially resentful Rory, three years her senior, who had been sent up to the crofthouse to bring her down. And by the time Gail had been old enough to understand, it had been too late to bring any comfort to that silent, beaten woman who dressed her in clean clothes, kept her fed and warm, as best she could, and painstakingly avoided looking at her. And in time she had come to understand that too.

Gail reached the straggle of farm buildings just as darkness began to lift and the day turned grey. Everyone would be up and about their chores, but she hoped, as she pushed open the back door, that she would find her uncle alone. With him, there would be no need to explain the sudden decision to visit her old school friend Kirsty Campbell, on the other side of the island. Instinctively she backed away, but her granny's malevolent gaze transfixed her on the threshold.

'So her ladyship has deigned to join us for breakfast,' the old lady sneered.

It was an old, well-worn tack: Gail thought herself no better than her kinfolk, but her grandmother had always resented the unconscious refinement that set Gail apart from the rest of her family.

'Good morning, Granny,' she forced out the placatory greeting, wondering if it made her a hypocrite, and smiled briefly at her uncle when his anxious eyes lifted from his bowl of steaming porridge.

'"All wickedness is but little to the wickedness of a woman",' Granny Mackenzie delivered sanctimoniously, nodding her grey hair with an air of great wisdom.

Gail was accustomed to her granny's biblical quotes offered at random and sounding sacrilegious on her uncharitable lips, but this one was said with a directness that implied a definite reason behind it. She attempted to ignore it, but Peggy Mackenzie had the bit between her teeth.

'Has your fancy man deserted you already?' she crowed. 'What comes cheap is valued as worthless—but you should have learned that by now.'

Fancy man?—Kyle Saunderson, no doubt. He had called in at the farm on his way up to the cottage. Her grandmother was wildly off target, as usual.

'He was a friend from Edinburgh—just a friend,' Gail tried to correct the mistaken impression, but her lie rang false.

'Now, Mother, let her be. That's what the gentleman said and that's how it is,' her uncle stepped in to rescue the niece of whom he was very fond.

'Hold your tongue, Calum!' Granny Mackenzie snapped. 'If you'd let me beat the wantonness out of her, she'd not have gone the way of her mother and be bringing shame on us now!'

It was more than Gail could bear this morning, and she

fled to the cowshed, sagging down on a bale of hay.

'I'm not like that. Am I?' She spoke her insecurity aloud, but got no comfort from her other self, who reminded her pointedly of her affair with a married man. She had not known the truth until it was too late, but, to Gail, there were no degrees of adultery. She had been prepared to do anything to make it up to Barry's wife and in the end followed the only course possible, although it seemed desperately inadequate. She had walked out on Barry, borne and given away their child on her own, and kept silent, hoping and praying that his wife would remain in ignorance.

It appeared that had been a vain hope, for Kyle Saunderson had said a divorce had followed, and perhaps it was time she accepted that she really was the person her granny had always seen her as—wanton and wicked and destructive. But that was by her own reasoning, not through her granny or through Kyle Saunderson.

The dairy cattle, although not a mainstay of the farm, were kept for milk for the family and a few crofters on the higher ground who dealt exclusively in sheep, but their number did not warrant any expensive electric machinery. Armed with bucket and three-legged stool, Gail tackled the job she had done countless times. She worked quickly, her fingers nimble with experience, emptying each bucketful into the large metal churn at the end of the byre.

He stepped out of the shadows just as she was tipping the last milk into the container, and although the cry of fright caught in her throat, the bucket slipped from her hands, spilling its contents over the stone floor.

'Damn, damn,' she muttered, temper replacing the initial shock. 'Look what you made me do!'

Kyle Saunderson did not reply but stood stock still, watching as she ineffectively mopped up the spilt milk with some straw. Her mind raced to assimilate the fact he had turned up at the farm an hour earlier than he had been due at the cottage, and to work out just how she was going to get away from him with the minimum of fuss and bother. Straightening up she tossed back her hair and glared at him. 'What are you doing here?' As she recognised the crumpled paper he drew from the side pocket of his waisted brown suede jacket, her, 'You're trespassing!' was more bluff than boldness.

'"Changed my mind. Send me the papers",' he read her blunt, short note, heavily stressing each syllable. 'You're certainly working with the right animals, you rude little . . .'

'If you don't get out of here, I'll call my uncle and he'll throw you off his land!' she stormed back, well aware of the name he had been about to apply to her.

Booted feet set slightly apart, with his hands resting on lean hips, he did not appear remotely ruffled by the threat. Gail took in his arrogant stance, the ruthless set of his firm, square jaw, and the straight humourless mouth . . . Her brain told her to run, but before she had even reached the door, he had caught her roughly by one arm, pivoting her round and she lost her footing; she winced with pain as her shoulder hit full force on the stone wall that broke her fall. But if Kyle was conscious of her hurt, he ignored it, his grip bruising as he held her pinned there.

'Let me go,' she spat at him, angry with herself for being afraid of him, and misguidedly crying out, 'or I'll . . .'

'You'll what, Miss Mackenzie?' he taunted. His hold tightened further, making her shoulder throb and she closed her eyes to the pain of it. When she opened them again, he was appraising her flushed cheeks and trembling bottom lip with that slow, insulting movement of narrowed grey eyes which made her flesh crawl.

He *was* enjoying it—the physical power he had over her.

'Go to hell!' she gritted through fiercely clenched teeth. Staring, with a mixture of fright and fascination, at the large hand poised to strike, Gail made no move to avoid it, but the blow never came, his fist was sent suddenly slamming against the wall behind her head, and the moment she found herself free of him she made another desperate dash for the door.

Sheer blind panic had her stumbling across the yard to the garaging, which consisted of a corrugated iron roof set on four steel girders, but without walls. The Land Rover was there, but so was Rory.

'Have you finished?' Gail urged, struggling to control her laboured breathing.

Her cousin, his carrot-red head bent over the engine, pointedly ignored her. Despair rose—she sensed Rory to be in one of his blank, unreachable moods.

'I need it now,' she pleaded, impulsively clutching at his arm. Violently he recoiled from her touch, as though it burned him, and spun round to face her. 'Please, Rory!'

As children they had been each other's confidents, fiercely loyal in their cousinship, and when Gail had come to stay after her mother's death, their relationship had subtly altered in a way she had been too young to fully comprehend. Grim-faced, he had listened to her news that one of the Easter visitors was prepared to give her a chance to sing professionally, sure that she would be home within a month. When she had eventually returned over a year later, it was to discover their old easy friendship shattered by the disgrace of her pregnancy, and that visit had been as brief as it had been painful. And now, with her back permanently on the island, Rory's behaviour varied with his moods—sometimes he treated her with the old tenderness, but most times with cutting scorn.

'Ask your fine English gentleman to fix it!' he blazed, throwing his spanner to the ground.

Gail glanced nervously in the direction of Rory's furious gaze, and there he was, standing about twenty yards away as if he had every right to be there.

'Rory, please, it's not what you think.' With her eyes she begged him to listen, not to condemn as he had before, without giving her a chance to explain.

The raking look of utter contempt warned her that his ever-ready temper was about to boil over, and this was confirmed by the ugly stream of abuse he threw at her in the first language of their Island grandparents. It was not the first time she had heard the brutally cruel words he used to express his opinion of her, but, from him, they still had the power to crush. She did not try to stem the damning flow, but stood meekly taking it all, Rory's clenched fists and anguished eyes telling her it was hurting him too. She choked back a sob which started her cough again, and for a second his arms reached involuntarily to her. And then, despising his weakness, he brushed past her, stalking away to the house.

'You don't appear to be over-popular here either,' Kyle Saunderson drawled to her back as she leaned her head against the side window. Once again she had not noticed his approach; for a big man he moved very quickly.

Scrambling into the Land Rover, she turned the ignition key left in the steering column, and for one glorious moment the engine revved into life, but before she could engage the lowest gear, it abruptly cut. Head down, she clicked the ignition switch on and off, refusing to accept that it would not fire again. The slamming of the bonnet brought her head up, and there he stood, in front of the windscreen, black head thrown back with mocking, triumphant laughter. Gail's fingers convulsively gripped the steering wheel as he came round to the driver's side. Childishly she went to lock the door on him, but he forestalled her, with one deft movement opening and throwing it wide.

'It's exceedingly dangerous to drive with the bonnet up,' he pointed out, 'and almost impossible without this.' He swung the distributor cap from one of its leads, but she resisted the temptation to snatch it from his hand, realising he would find her attempt to refit it even more amusing. Turning in her seat, she prepared to jump down, but his leaning on the inside of the door barred her exit.

'No, I think I prefer you sitting there for the moment. I don't particularly enjoy keeping up with the antics of a recalcitrant child.'

'Age will tell,' she muttered nastily and unfairly. He was in superb physical condition, without an ounce of spare flesh on his muscular frame; he observed her interest, and she quickly averted her eyes.

'You and the young farmer certainly have the temper to match your colouring,' he drawled.

'You heard?'

'My Gaelic repertoire includes just three words—*"ceud mille faite"*—a thousand welcomes—and something tells me that phrase didn't crop up in the conversation. I would like a translation. Now.' He had reverted to being the impossible, domineering male.

'It's none of your business, Mr Saunderson.' No anger this time, but she meant it.

'As my presence obviously prompted the "discussion", I think it is. So I want to hear it, word for word,' he rapped out. He waited, and when she made no effort to answer, he added insidiously, 'Or I could go back and ask the young man?'

He backed a fraction away, and Gail grabbed his arm. Jet black eyebrows lifted in mock enquiry and it was a struggle not to obey the impulse to slap his arrogant face. She thought she had bettered him by leaving the cottage before sunrise, but she had landed herself in a more unpalatable situation. She said tonelessly, 'I don't think you should do that.'

'Why not?' he asked, a smile playing on his lips.

'I'm asking you not to.' It was extremely galling to have

to ask this man for anything, and to her own ears the request sounded forced and ungracious.

'Try asking harder.' He was determined to extract his full pound of flesh, making her pay for her attempt to outmanoeuvre him.

She swallowed hard, and lowering her head so that her face was concealed by her wild, unkept hair, she sought the right note of supplication.

'I'm asking you not to go near Rory . . . please!'

A strong brown hand roughly jerked her chin up, and lingered there while he read the defiant expression that denied the sincerity of her tone. 'You have a choice—either you tell me what was said or I go and ask him.'

He'd asked for it. 'Word for word?' she threw at him. He nodded. 'He told me to get the father of my bastard brat off this land or he'd kick him off,' she said in a flat, distinct tone that concealed all the hurt Rory's speech had inflicted. 'Ridiculous, isn't it?'

'That he thinks I'm the father of the child you bore?'

'That he would actually believe that I would be attracted to someone like you,' she taunted, her foolish pride getting in the way of common sense.

Surprisingly he seemed more furious at her remark than he had been at Rory's misassumption. 'What else did he say?'

Wasn't that enough for him? 'That I was a whoring bitch on heat for a male.' Gail kept her voice steady, determined to cheat him out of her pain. 'The rest was roughly on the same lines.'

Kyle's nostrils flared, betraying an anger she didn't understand. 'And you stood there and took it all, when you would have scratched my eyes out for the same?'

'Rory's my cousin.'

'And that gives him the right,' he muttered disbelievingly.

'Yes.'

'And because it's true,' he said with conviction.

She would not allow this supercilious Englishman to sit in judgment over her. 'On this island, a woman is a whore if she sleeps with a man before marriage. If that's your definition, then yes, I am one.'

Unconsciously he clawed a hand through his thick black hair, and with it disarranged he looked younger, almost approachable.

The shrewdness of his next question startled her. 'Is that why you gave up the baby? So that blind prejudice wouldn't touch him?'

He had drawn closer until they were a whisper away from touching, and Gail had the crazy urge to rest her head on his broad shoulder, to seek refuge there from the cruelty of life. At the last moment she pulled herself up, visibly stiffening; hadn't she learned enough about life yet to be so easily lulled by the softness that had crept into his voice? 'You credit me with finer feelings I don't possess,' she declared derisively. 'We've already established that I'm rotten to the core.'

'You don't give anything away, do you?' he rasped, any hint of warmth fast disappearing. 'I wonder if the air of aloofness is surface deep.'

'Believe me, underneath this cold exterior lies a solid block of ice,' she parried, bent on distancing him emotionally, if not physically, but he laughed outright at her bold claim to invulnerability.

'Ice melts.'

'Not if it's kept at a constantly cold temperature,' she said, adding silently, 'and never for you.'

'Perhaps a warmer climate will bring out a thaw,' he returned with the air of gaining satisfaction from their sparring, probably confident he would prove more than a match for her. He consulted his watch. 'We should just make the morning ferry.'

His arrogance, as natural to him as breathing, had

reasserted itself, but Gail welcomed it as something she could rail against. 'I haven't said I'm leaving.'

He stepped back from the Land Rover and his disparaging glance swept the farmyard, taking in the grim exterior of the ramshackle farmhouse, as cheerless outside as in, scattered pieces of machinery, abandoned when no longer useful, and the ugly, crumbling outbuildings, not improved by the blanket of snow. 'Is there anything . . . anyone here for you, Gail Mackenzie?' he asked.

Face it, he was saying. And she did: she had returned to the island, hoping to do penance by helping on the farm, but it had been futile. There wasn't a home for her here any more; there never really had been.

'No. No, there isn't,' she admitted. She bit back tears of self-pity and the effort to swallow the lump in her throat started her coughing once more, leaving her drained when the fit subsided.

Kyle was studying her flushed cheeks, but made no move to stop her getting down from the Land Rover. 'My car's parked on the other side of the house.'

'I'll have to get my bag.' She had dumped it on the kitchen floor.

'Be quick!' he called out to her retreating back.

Gail was surprised her uncle was not out on the hills by this relatively late hour, but it became obvious from his words, more statement than question, that he had been waiting for her, perhaps watching her encounter with Kyle Saunderson.

'You're off, then.'

'There's nothing for me here, Uncle Calley,' she repeated, without accusation, the conviction Kyle Saunderson had helped formed in her mind.

'No, child, there's not,' he agreed reluctantly. He'd miss her sorely, the only reminder of his pretty little sister who had left the island to escape their mother's influence and returned to pay a hundredfold for that brief freedom.

And that was that; they both knew she wouldn't be back this time. She was at the door, bag clutched under the arm of her parka, when he stopped her. Placing a large, work-coarsened hand on her head, he ruffled her hair, an affection almost forgotten from childhood.

'My bonnie, bonnie bairn,' he hoarsely gave his blessing.

Gail checked the impulse to throw herself into his arms; they were a family not given to displays of tender emotion, but for a second she held his fingers tightly, transmitting her message of love.

When she rounded the corner of the house, Kyle Saunderson was noisily revving the engine, impatient to be gone. She circled round to the passenger door, and he stretched over and pushed it open. Noticing the immaculate floor carpeting, she hesitated.

'For Pete's sake, get in,' he ordered with rising exasperation.

'My boots,' she protested, lifting the far from clean wellingtons for his inspection, and he heaved a sigh that brought a quick scowl to her face.

'The carpet can stand it. You can change back at your cottage. You do have shoes, I presume,' he added sarcastically.

Gail did not bother replying. It was a long way to London and it was up to one of them to behave with some measure of dignity if the journey was to be at all tolerable. Instead she concentrated on clinging to her seat to keep upright, because the car was sliding dramatically from side to side as they climbed.

When they reached the cottage, her nerves were jangling, and her hands fumbled incompetently with the door catch. Again a heavy sigh spoke of Kyle's growing irritation, but she had not anticipated him leaning over to help her. His body pressed against the curve of her breasts and she instinctively drew back from the intimate contact and the distinctly male smell of aftershave and tobacco. The gesture did not pass unnoticed, and his lips formed a thin line, but instead of pulling away, he kept his hand on the door, preventing her alighting. Purposefully he leaned even closer, watching her reaction and flaring with anger when she shrank further into the soft leather upholstery.

'You really do find my touch repulsive, don't you?' he grated harshly.

Her mind ordered her to stay silent, to let him keep thinking that, while her heart pounded erratically with a sensation that was both chaotic and alarming. She shut her eyes to block out the image of the dark head that loomed menacingly over hers, praying the waves of desire would pass from her when she was no longer able to see the features that were, at times, so hauntingly like Barry's. Violently Kyle wrenched open the door, uncaring of the hard pressure he exerted on her much smaller frame, and all but pushed her out of the car.

'Get out before you're sick in the car,' he muttered disgustedly, and then when she quickly scrambled out, he ordered, 'Ten minutes.'

Gail caught her reflection in the hall mirror—white and wild-eyed. No wonder he had thought her on the verge of being ill! Hurriedly she packed one battered suitcase, selecting the few clothes that were clean and undarned, left the crofthouse as it stood and walked away without looking over her shoulders. It was stone and wood, nothing more.

Kyle was leaning against the boot, arms folded across his wide expanse of chest, and his mouth quirked with annoyance when he spotted the second case she was carrying.

'What's that?' he said stonily.

Of course he knew what it was; it was his way of showing further contempt.

'A rather large violin,' Gail replied airily.

In response to her impudence, he threw the case forcibly into the spacious boot, careless of any damage he might cause to the delicate strings of the guitar contained in the black, scuffed case—and Gail's dislike began to crystallise into hate.

CHAPTER FOUR

If this was how she felt after a bare three hours of his company, what would she feel in a day or two?—murderous, she predicted, as she slammed the door behind her and put as much distance between the blue Ferrari and herself as was possible on the ferryboat. The brooding silence she could stand, even welcome, but Kyle Saunderson punctuated it with snide, hurting remarks as though he wished to punish her for some unutterable crime. Gail couldn't believe that a hardened cynic like him would really care about the fate of a child who, as far as he was concerned, was no longer related to him; she had promised to give up her claim to his precious business. So why was he using her as a whipping boy, treating her with a searing contempt that was out of all proportion to the situation?

Gripping the rail, she steadied herself as the boat lurched forward. The hills that rose above the harbour were blanketed with snow; it presented a pretty Christmas-card scene, but she wished her last image of the island, the one she would carry with her always, could have been of its green and bracken-brown splendour in early autumn, before November gales made it an austere, forbidding place once more. Perhaps it was better she left while there was a bitter wind chasing through her clothes, making her wrap her navy duffle coat tighter round her: it would be less of a temptation to falsely sentimentalise.

Not wanting to go below deck and risk the ignominy of being ill, because the sea was far from calm, Gail remained at the rails staring out at the harbour and the lone figure that stood, motionless, at the edge of the wharf. Had she not recognised the sheep lorry that had drawn up as the ferry pulled away from shore, she would have known him by the red hair, as unruly as her own, that was like a banner. Incredible that he had come, and even more unbelievable when his hand rose and was held steadily in the air. It was a salute of farewell, and she did not imagine it to be anything else, but it suffused her chilled body with a warmth that radiated from the ungloved hand she lifted, her fingers spreading as though to meet him across the water.

'How touching!' The moment was shattered by the harsh cynicism, and Gail wanted to cry over the pieces. 'A lover's farewell?'

'Does being obnoxious come naturally to you, Mr Saunderson, or do you have to work at it?'

'No denial, I see.'

'Would there be any point?'

'No, none at all,' he affirmed. 'While you were in the house fetching your bag, your cousin took the opportunity to give me some free advice. Namely if I were to hurt one hair on your precious head, he would come looking for me with a twelve-bore shotgun. Very dramatic for just a cousin, wouldn't you say?'

'Rory and I—we were fond of each other when we were kids,' she said distractedly, turning away from him to gaze over once more to the island, but the engulfing sea mist cheated her of a last sight of her cousin whose loyalty had overridden his bitterness.

'Fond!' Kyle repeated, with harsh disbelief, spinning her round to face him.

'Yes, you know—affection. I'm sure you've read about such an emotion,' she countered, leaving him in no doubt that she believed him incapable of experiencing it, and knowing by the tightening, bruising grip on her upper arms, she was succeeding in goading him.

'Did you enjoy keeping the poor fool dangling? Is that

how you get your kicks?' His voice had dropped to a low, insulting drawl.

'We were friends, that's all,' she opposed hotly.

'The same way you and my brother were. You still had a hold on him in the end too.' His eyes moved from her face, down the length of her figure made shapeless by her thick clothing. 'You must have hidden talents.'

'I'm extremely flattered that you see me as a femme fatale, but you couldn't be more wrong about Rory. If he'd been in love with me, he wouldn't have . . .' she trailed off, wanting to bite her rash, betraying tongue.

'He wouldn't have turned on you when you returned from Edinburgh,' Kyle finished for her, with an accuracy that was uncanny. 'Are you really so naïve? No man wants shopsoiled goods, especially if he'd set his mind on being the first. And believe me, your cousin saw himself in that role.'

His cruel, taunting 'shop-soiled' cut through her defences, piercing a core that was still vulnerable in its softness. He made her feel momentarily unclean—and then pride had her re-surfacing, flashing bright on her upturned face, as she retorted coolly, 'What makes you think he wasn't?'

'What do you mean?' he demanded savagely.

'Aren't you being naïve now, Mr Saunderson? I went to live on the farm when I was fifteen. Rory and I often played in the hayloft. I'm sure you get the picture.' With sly insinuation she had painted it well enough, even if it was a gross distortion of the true image of her innocent childhood. 'And you're quite right, I do have hidden talents.'

'I just bet you have!' It was not meant to be a compliment. 'Your type of woman has but one use, Miss Mackenzie.'

Gail almost laughed at the ludicrousness of it—fury written on every harsh line, and vibrating through every

quietly-spoken syllable—and he still addressed her formally, as if they were polite strangers! Instead she
assumed a false lightness. 'Let me guess. I can't cook very
well, so, in your book, that leaves only one other function I
could possibly perform, doesn't it?' She threw him what
she hoped would pass for a look of sexual provocation,
quite carried away by the part she was playing and certain
of the effect it would have—to disgust him further,
perhaps have him recoiling from her with the idea she had
designs on him too.

Mesmerised by the frank, startling desire reflected in
dark grey eyes, Gail made no move to check the hand that
curled round her nape and seductively stroked the soft
skin that lay under the swathe of thick waving hair.

'If that's an offer, I could be interested—at the right
price,' he murmured low in his throat. 'It's always better
with a woman who knows how to please a man.'

'I . . . I . . .' she stuttered her confusion, unconsciously
running the tip of her tongue over dry, nervous lips that
refused to articulate her horrified reaction.

'And knows how to turn him on,' he groaned, his eyes
following the movement.

The fingers curling round her neck abandoned their
sensual caress as they jerked her head up to meet his
swooping, predatory mouth. His kiss was a brutal assault,
his mouth grinding against her clenched teeth in an
attempt to force a greater intimacy. When she would have
twisted her head away, he gripped a handful of hair and
held it steady, at the same time biting into the flesh of her
upper lip. Gail opened her lips to cry out, more in shock
than pain, and forcing her against the railing, Kyle used
the advantage it gave to deepen the kiss, plundering the
sweetness exposed to his searching, rapacious mouth.
And penetrating through her fear and anger came a sweet,
clamouring excitement as the pressure of his mouth subtly
altered to a kiss that sought to devastate with its seductive

expertise, its promise of sensual pleasure that had her fighting herself as well as him, struggling with her mind to resist the urge of her body to answer his passion with a long-dormant one of her own.

On the verge of surrendering in a fight that no longer seemed important, her salvation came in the form of Kyle Saunderson's sudden pushing her away. Any relief at finding herself free was secondary to the confusing sense of loss. Tentatively she fingered her throbbing lips and found them wet with blood, and her blue eyes, wide and accusing, dominated her pale, frightened face.

'You're not quite ready to play with the grown-ups, are you?' he mocked her panic.

His expression was devoid of emotion but inside he was laughing at her, at her pretence to a worldliness that he had shown up to be a complete sham. Blinding fury drove her hand up to crack hard on his cheek, but she derived no satisfaction from the blow that did not even cause him to wince. It was hollow revenge, for his steady gaze told her he had expected it, and had not bothered to avoid it.

'Temper tantrums at your age?' he commented mildly, casually shoving his hands into his trouser pockets.

Frustration welled up inside her at her inability to get at him in any way while he had wreaked havoc with one kiss. It seemed as if he was reading her mind when he continued with, 'You act as though you've never been kissed before.'

'I have—thousands of times.' It sounded like childish boasting and had his hateful mouth quirking into an amused smile.

'Methinks the lady doth protest too much,' he quoted softly, laughter in his voice and his eyes, lightened to a warm grey. Gail fought to keep cool, not trusting her voice to be steady enough to reply. 'Those baby-blue eyes tell me you want to take another swipe at me, so I think I'll move temptation out of your way.'

And so saying, he turned on his heel and walked towards the stern of the ferryboat, back to his car.

Infuriating, insufferable, loathsome! she muttered to herself in the absence of the object of her scorn. She didn't know which was worse—his treating her like a naughty, bad-tempered child, or her reacting like one. Where had all her determination to act with cool restraint gone?—dissolved by a kiss that had been no token of love, but an appeal to a much more basic, primitive emotion.

If Kyle had not, with cold deliberation, spoilt the moment for her, she would have remembered her leaving the island with some small degree of pleasure from the knowledge that Rory had, in the end, cared enough to say goodbye. Now she would recall that deep, probing kiss that had nearly drawn a response from her own lips and made her body alive to a need in her. Was it for the long-forgotten joy of loving or simply for the sensuous enjoyment of physical lovemaking? Either way, it was a need that would have to go unsatisfied. She didn't require Kyle Saunderson to point out that the permissive era of the early seventies had done little, if anything, to weaken the double standard for men and women in the matter of sexual freedom. Not only in his cold, censuring eyes was she sentenced for giving herself to a man who could not possibly have made her his wife. That she had been unaware she had been playing the part of the much-despised other woman was completely irrelevant.

Her thoughts drifted once more back over the years . . .

When they had left that railway carriage, Gail knew all she thought she needed to know about Barry Saunderson. He was thirty—information supplied with a rueful grimace—working as a political correspondent for a national paper, currently in Edinburgh for the background to the issue of devolution for Scotland, and he was, without doubt, the most fascinating, wonderful human being she had ever met. With a professional talent for storytelling and a total refusal to take life at all seriously, he dispelled Gail's almost painful shyness, and made her experience a new confidence in herself. Perhaps she was a person worth knowing, after all.

He insisted on carrying her luggage when they reached their destination, and guarding their bags while he looked for an available taxi, Gail felt that someone, after neglecting her for so long, had decided to give her all her chances for happiness at this one time of her life—the opportunity to sing at a popular city folk-club despite her lack of any real experience, and now superseding it, making it seem a bonus rather than the most important thing in her young life, Barry Saunderson. It appeared too good to be true.

And it was. Seated alone in the back of a taxi, she cursed herself for her naïvety (or was it conceit?), in believing that she could attract the handsome, witty journalist. He installed her in the taxi, held her hand for a few breathless seconds and then stood waving as the cab pulled up the ramp out of the underground taxi rank—but there had been no request for her address or telephone number, no indication of wishing to see her again. She feld idiotic as the tears streamed down her face the length of Princes Street for a man she had known for a few short hours.

The next night she gave her first professional performance in 'Country Folk' and when, having completed her repertoire of traditional Scottish ballads, she came off the small, raised platform in the centre of the club room, she knew herself a failure. Her voice, usually so clear and pure, had faltered every time she caught the eye of any customer, and her fingers had taken the dimensions of thumbs as she accompanied herself on the guitar. When one of the waiters knocked on her tiny dressing-room door with the message that the manager wanted to see her, it came as no surprise, and crying inside with the loneliness that only two days in a big, alien city can cause, she almost welcomed the idea that her services were no longer required.

But Peter Mason, manager and owner, had more confidence than she felt she warranted and the expected dismissal never came. Within a fortnight, equipped with a brand new guitar, far superior to her first, and bolstered by Peter's determination to make a competent, if not outstanding, professional singer, Gail was singing with the slightly wistful, pure-noted quality that had attracted the manager's attention when he had been holidaying on the west coast, and actually gathering a following among devotees of Scottish folk music. While Gail improved nightly, Peter made more extravagant plans for her until, realising it wasn't all banter to encourage her, she had to put a damper on his enthusiasm. Gail loved singing, and, although she seldom felt fully relaxed in front of an audience, took pleasure in the fact she entertained people, but there was no way she ever wanted to claw her way to the top of her field, in a business that was as hard as it was fickle; she neither had the ambition nor the necessary self-absorption to be a success on a national, far less international, scale. With evident disappointment but a measure of good grace, he cancelled his arrangements with a recording studio to whom he had sent a cassette tape of her singing.

It was normal for Gail to concentrate on her singing and playing, knowing her early mistakes had been caused by an embarrassed awareness of her audience. It was pure chance, therefore, that she noticed his presence at all in the dimly-lit basement club. She was announcing the background to her next song, at the same time trying to change the key of her instrument without attracting too much attention, when she was momentarily distracted by the scraping of a chair at one of the tables nearest her rostrum. And there he was—seated directly in front of her, as disarmingly handsome as she remembered—and her hands became frozen on the guitar strings, her voice dried up to a whisper. Her first impulse was of annoyance: she had almost forgotten the charming stranger from the train, and now he had spoilt all her efforts to relegate their meeting to an unimportant incident. The murmurs of an audience growing restless enabled her to drag her eyes away from Barry Saunderson, but it took a number of false starts to get into the number she had just introduced, and she caught the worried glance of Peter Mason as he stood chatting to his customers at the bar.

The sense that she was letting him down carried her through the next two songs, determinedly preoccupying herself with the deft movement of her fingers on the frets of the guitar. And then, in the middle of a plaintive lovesong of another century, her traitor eyes wandered back to him, and the warm, teasing light of slate-grey eyes compelled her not to look away. The impression that every joy-filled note was sung from him alone persisted to the end of her performance.

For a week he came, night after night, occupying the nearest vacant table to the stage, listening to her while she sang only for him, but leaving without making any verbal contact with her. During the day Gail looked on his coming as something unreal, out of a soap opera fantasy, but at night her eyes searched the tables, reassuring herself with his presence. The two days he failed to appear caused her singing to take on a monotonous quality, while she struggled to fight back the waves of crushing disappointment that washed over her, but she made up for her lacklustre performance on the third night when he returned. This time he did not allow her to disappear backstage, and Gail did not pretend she was anything but eager to sit with him.

It became a routine, never discussed but implicitly agreed, that he would arrive during her performance, listen to the music and then walk her home to her bedsit, their footsteps dragging slower and slower with time passing. And one night, filled with love and being in love, she had not gone home at all. She had been scared, and Barry had been infinitely tender, and when morning brought regrets and doubts, he had cradled her in his arms and smothered them with soft, loving phrases till they were reduced to a small whisper of conscience.

When he had asked her to live with him, strangely the decision to do so had been clear-cut. Rightly or wrongly, Gail had already committed herself to him, outside marriage. The time since their meeting had been short, measured in weeks and days, but long enough for dreams. Impossible and foolish, so fragile they could disappear in the space between two heartbeats.

And yet the memory of that happiness somehow remained as real, as right . . .

'Dreaming of a tall, dark and handsome man?'

Too absorbed with the past to notice the boat was coming into the new harbour at Ullapool, Gail reddened at the thought of how wistful her expression must have been.

'I've had enough, more than enough, of tall, dark and handsome men to last me a lifetime,' she returned bitterly. She would scream the next time Kyle crept silently up to her in order to deliver some derisive comment—not with fright but pure Celtic temper.

'I'm most flattered you find me handsome,' he laughed, knowing without conceit she had been referring to him.

'Doubtlessly some fool women find your brand of looks and unabounding masculine arrogance an utterly thrilling combination!'

'But not you, Gail?'

'Certainly not!' she immediately denied. 'And no one said you could use my first name!'

'My apologies, little ginger cat.' He spoke in a tone that he would use to a small child.

'My hair is not ginger, and cats do not have blue eyes,' Gail declared caustically.

With one finger he flicked off the hood of her duffel coat and pretended to assess her colouring, with an exaggerated seriousness. 'Well, I would say it definitely has a fiery red in it. And as for the second part, I wasn't alluding to those deceptively innocent-looking eyes.'

The foot passengers emerging from the enclosed travelling cabin acted as a restraint to any urge to violence, and she announced tautly, with the air of one who is bestowing a great honour, 'When you need to address me, and I hope the occasions will be rare, you have my permission to call me Gail, Mr Saunderson.'

He laughed outright, more with humour than hard mockery, and she stamped on the notion that it was a pleasing, attractive sound. 'You have all the haughtiness of a great lady. Perhaps,' he added, in the manner of someone enjoying a private joke with himself, 'you should set your sights on ensnaring a member of the aristocracy.'

'I have no interest in any man who can only gain respect, self or otherwise, from being born with a position in an outdated feudal system and a silver spoon stuck so far into his mouth that he's prevented from speaking normally!'

She had thought to score points against this Englishman, knowing his nation had more than a passing reverence for their titles, but it seemed, if the slow smile that softened his features was to be taken at face value, she had actually, somehow, pleased him. Gail felt bewildered—all morning they had been striking sparks off each other, vying to be the more insulting, and now she did not seem to be managing to penetrate his darkly tanned skin one inch.

'Then you're the exception.'

'That proves the rule,' she finished for him. 'Anyway, it wouldn't matter if I did set my sights, would it?'

'Why?' he smiled down at her.

'As you so accurately pointed out earlier, no man is going to buy my shopsoiled wares.' Gail affected a hard carelessness in repeating the cruel jibe to its originator. A muscle throbbed at his temple line and she congratulated herself on finally annoying him; inexplicably she felt much safer when their conversation was vitriolic with their mutual dislike.

But his next, quiet statement suggested she had misinterpreted the erratic movement.

'I hope you will accept my sincere apology for words intended to hurt but not to be taken literally. Any man . . .'

'You don't have to dress up the truth for me. I'm quite capable of taking it,' Gail cut in, knocking away the hand that was resting lightly on her shoulder. She was on to his latest ploy—charm the simple little Scottish girl into total acquiescence with a few meaningless smiles and an easy apology. And he was good at it, the contrition in the arch of his black eyebrows was almost convincing. But not quite good enough!

He prevented her from turning away from him and looked unruffled by her show of aggression. 'Perhaps I can take it too—why don't you try me, Gail?'

Gail understood. He was offering her a chance to give her account of the past. Try him—trust him? She glanced up at him and the smile of encouragement forming on his lips had a contrary effect on her highly suspicious mind.

'You already have it taped and catalogued, Mr Saunderson, under "a" for affair. Or perhaps "s" for sordid?' she stated loftily, and moved to brush past him.

'Damn you, Gail Mackenzie, and your stiff-necked pride!' he growled down at her, trapping her at his side.

'You're hurting me!' she gasped.

'Where do you think you're going?'

'Nowhere,' she answered nervously. The way he was looking at her—it was frightening. He didn't seem to be aware of the excessive pressure of his hand on her upper arm, as though all his energy, mental and physical, was directed at holding on to her.

And then the next moment he was all suavity, chatting casually with the ferry skipper who had unknowingly broken the tension with his request for them to move their vehicle so they could begin to load the cars waiting on the quay. It was obvious that the ferryman took them for newly-marrieds, too involved in each other to notice the boat had docked, and Kyle Saunderson played along with the impression as he curved his arm lightly round her shoulders.

'I think I'll walk along to the old pier.' Gail wasn't ready to climb back into a car with a man who had been close to breaking her arm. She was still shaking inside.

'Gail!' It was a caution. Any more he would have said was inhibited by the presence of the affable skipper.

'I'll meet you there,' she mumbled something approaching a promise and took to her heels the instant his arm dropped away, the men's laughter following her as she hurried down the passenger ramp.

Gail forced herself to walk away from the new harbour down the main street, although she had a crazy urge to break into a run. Crazy, because, as she had admitted to Kyle, there was nowhere to run to. She couldn't go back to the island, and she had virtually no money to go elsewhere. And why should she want to run anyway? She slowed down some more. One provoked, the other reacted—it was already the pattern set in their short acquaintanceship. Nothing had changed. A slight over-reaction, that was all.

She reached the fishing pier and briefly looked back. The blue Ferrari was nowhere in sight, and she was relieved. They both needed time to cool down. She walked to the end of the pier, picturesque in summer with greedy gulls circling for the chance of some free dinner, and the bright sunlight dancing on the clear water as the fishermen, joking among themselves, briskly unloaded their catch. Today it was different: what little catch had been lifted from the unfriendly gale-torn waters had long since been taken from the holds of the few boats in the harbour, and the chilling emptiness of the near-deserted fishing village made a mockery of the pretty postcard views that were representative of less than five months of the year.

Gail stared down at the water; it was murky and held traces of oil leaking from one of the diesel-driven boats. The wind from the sea was whipping through her hair, pulling it back from her scalp, and her ears began hurting with the cold. In fact if she stood there much longer, she wouldn't just have cooled down—she'd be frozen over!

Head down against the wind, she retraced her steps and blindly cannoned into the fisherman who had been weaving his way back to a boat, equally oblivious to traffic coming from the opposite direction. Despite his bulk, it was Gail who ended up steadying them both from the impact when she caught the familiar odour of whisky. She stepped back a pace and her face instantly formed a smile of recognition for the ruddy-complexioned man, dressed in traditional cableknit sweater and thick work cords.

'It's yourself, Donald!'

A slow, abashed grin spread over his weatherbeaten face. 'Aye.'

'How are you?' Gail asked, confronted with a shyness that had always been more painful than her own. They had been to school together, but in her semi-isolation on the island she hadn't seen him in years.

'Slightly under the weather, I'm afraid,' he muttered, his voice thick with the drink. 'And yourself?'

'Fine,' she responded, deciding against removing the

support she was lending him. 'Still on your father's boat?'

'Aye.' He nodded slowly. 'But they're bitter cold, the nights.'

She didn't have to imagine how cold it could be out on the Minch; once she had gone out for a whole night on the herring fishing before it was suspended, and once was more than enough.

They both heard his father calling to him from the cockpit of the Mackay family boat, his voice harsh with anger at his son's condition, and they wished each other a hasty goodbye, although Donald gave her another of his lazy grins that told her that his father's wrath would be ineffectual for a few hours at least.

For no particular reason the incident cheered Gail up, and when she approached the Ferrari, now parked on the road beside the pier, she was still wearing the parting smile she had given Donald. Kyle Saunderson was leaning against the side of the car, and from his casual stance Gail deduced, with a measure of relief, that he too had regained his composure. Perhaps they could even establish a more civilised mode of behaviour towards each other.

How wrong she had been! If anything, he was angrier. She could have misinterpreted the look of intense dislike he directed towards her as she climbed into the passenger seat, but not the furious door slamming or the uncharacteristic crunching of gears before he proved that the car had alarmingly fast acceleration.

Well, she wasn't going to be the first to break the brooding silence that quickly developed and, she assured herself, she was completely indifferent to his savage mood.

Ten miles on, his taking of a sharp, unexpected bend at a reckless pace broke her resolve. 'OK, you've got me scared,' she cried shakily, and immediately regretted it. It sounded cowardly. With a contrived airiness, she ran on, '*I'm* too young to die, and suicide is a sin, you know!'

For a moment it appeared they were travelling even faster, and then the car mercifully slowed down to a speed more suitable for the extreme narrowness of the road.

'I bow to your superior first-hand knowledge of the subject,' Kyle responded, his lips barely moving.

Back to snide remarks, Gail commented to herself. She wasn't bothered by his acidity. So why couldn't she just let it go?

'Seasickness,' she queried with a false note of concern that he was meant to see right through, and did, if the white knuckles on the steering wheel were any indication.

'Disgust,' he threw at her, his eyes still rigid on the road ahead.

No prizes for guessing with whom, she thought wryly. 'If you have something to say, Mr Saunderson, I suggest you come right out with it. In my country we may understand but we do not appreciate the oblique remarks the English indulge in.'

She had not expected him to pull off the road into the next layby, and switching off the engine, swing round with a barely suppressed violence.

'All right, Miss Mackenzie,' he ground out, 'since you would appreciate plain speaking—while you're my passenger, I expect you to make an effort to control your natural impulses and behave with a measure of decorum, even when my back is turned.'

'Are you referring to Donald?' She spun round to face him, catching his drift despite the phrasing she considered to be anything but plain.

'If that's the name of your drunken friend,' he returned stiffly, and mistaking the sudden flush of red on her cheekbones, he added more insinuatingly, 'Or maybe he's another cousin of whom you're fond?'

'I don't believe this,' Gail cried indignantly. 'You, Mr Kyle Saunderson, have a mind comparable to a drainage system! You see me talking to an old school friend for a few

minutes, and straightaway you've transferred us to some
bedroom scene of your own lurid imagining! Is that how
you get your kicks?'

He perceptibly recoiled, but took her verbal lashing
without the swift retaliation she had anticipated. He sat
motionless, staring across at her, and she forced herself
not to look away from his searing, searching gaze.

'Maybe I was overhasty in my conclusions, but he was
obviously drunk and smiling at you with an unmistakable
lasciviousness,' he finally announced.

Was that meant to pass for an apology? Gail didn't
think so and made no effort to check her 'natural impulse'
to set this condescending Englishman straight about her
'drunken friend'. 'Have you ever been out all night in a
fishing boat with the wind from the Atlantic ripping
through your clothing, throwing the ocean at you and
making it a continuous battle to stay on your feet and out
of water? Because if you had, you might understand why
Donald was drunk at that time of day—to take the chill
from his bones and put the courage back into him to face
another night on the sea!' Gail's lilting accent became
more pronounced as she passionately defended the young
islander. 'And that grin you see as lascivious has been a
permanent feature on Donald Mackay's face since the day
we started school together. I was four and a half and he
was all of five.'

Kyle listened and at the end, said simply, 'Point taken.'

But that *was* meant as an apology, reinforced by the
silent message conveyed by the eyes holding hers. His
mouth was unsmiling, but the harshness had gone from
his strong, masculine features. He seemed sorry—very
sorry—as though the bitter exchange had affected him
too. Gail dropped her eyes away.

'You're very loyal to those you like, aren't you?'

His remark was charged with emotion, thick and distinct from any that had gone before. Too much emotion,

more real than the anger that had vibrated between them. Gail's fingers plucked nervously at the ribbing of the leather upholstery. 'He was just a boy I knew at school,' she stated without aggression.

'I'm not sure if I really believed anything worse,' he replied enigmatically, and Gail was conscious of him trying to tread softly as he explained, 'You *make* me do and say things, Gail. Do you understand that, I wonder?'

Yes, she understood. He did the same to her—caused her temper to rise and strike out blindly. He had given her an opportunity to resume the fight, but at that moment she could no longer remember why it was all necessary. She was tired. Too much emotion, her mind repeated its protest. She had to put distance between them. She leaned back on the headrest and stared out of the windscreen.

'It's snowing.'

Impersonal, trite, absurd in the context of the conversation, yet it snapped any link he had been trying to forge, just as it was intended to do. Gail caught his curse, low and almost inaudible beneath the abrupt firing of the engine, and felt, for some unfathomable reason, that she deserved it.

But she couldn't go back. He was no longer reaching out to her; the emotion had disappeared.

CHAPTER FIVE

Initially disorientated, Gail slowly realised she was lying almost horizontal, but not in her usual cold bed. Freeing her hands out of swathes of warm wool, she struggled to rise and the reclining seat came up with her. Mind still fuddled with sleep, she looked out into the night, trying to identify her surroundings—street lights and the range of multiple stores common to the built-up areas of any British city. How long had she slept? Kyle had stopped briefly in Inverness to buy some sandwiches. She had forced down one of the packets he had silently tossed into her lap and must have dozed off shortly afterwards. He had draped a travelling rug over her while she slept.

Gail swallowed a lump in her throat, feeling a raw ache at its base, but before she could find her voice to ask their whereabouts, the car had stopped briefly at a set of traffic lights and she saw an all too familiar landmark—the Scott Memorial dominating the floodlit Princes Street Gardens.

'We'll stay here tonight,' Kyle explained tonelessly, drawing the car to a halt.

'Couldn't we go on?' she urged, not considering her words or tone, only aware that she didn't want to spend any time in Edinburgh.

The inside of the car was partially illuminated by the light streaming from a glass-fronted hotel foyer, but his head was in shadow. Gail sensed rather than witnessed his irascibility with her truculent attitude.

'I've been driving for five hours. I'm hungry. I need a drink. And I have no intention of spending the rest of the evening finding somewhere else,' he declared uncompromisingly. 'So if you're worried about disturbing some

74

precious memories, you have my permission to pass the night in the car.'

'I don't understand what you mean.' Her head felt hot and heavy with sleep, and she was genuinely perplexed by the bitterness in his tone.

'Don't you? I think you *do*, Miss Mackenzie,' he adopted a deceptively soft note. 'I was quite familiar with my brother's style.'

'You think Barry used to take me here, to this hotel, for a meal,' she surmised belatedly.

'Oh, I wasn't thinking of anything so mundane as dinner,' Kyle delivered with a suggestiveness that was more than insolent.

And at last Gail was on his wavelength, receiving him loud and damnably clear. He imagined her affair with his brother to have been conducted on traditional lines— illicit meetings in hotel bedrooms. Well, let him think it; she didn't care to have his good opinion, did she?

'How astute of you, Mr Saunderson. And you're so right. Why should we go somewhere else when I have the chance to revive old times? I might even be given the same room where we used to . . .'

Gail didn't get the opportunity to finish her rash speech, but the slam of his door told her she had more than hit the target. He had given her the rod with which to beat him—for some reason, perhaps a puritanism that smacked of hypocrisy when she recalled that humiliating kiss on the boat, he hated the idea of her intimacy with Barry.

Her first impressions of the hotel lobby were consistent with the building's exterior—cheerless and utterly grand; she caught the suspicious glance of the liveried doorman, appraising her patently inexpensive clothing. A sense of mischief tempted her to tell him she was a millionairess in disguise, but the truth of it returned suddenly to shock her. How could she have forgotten that, for a few days anyway, she was a very wealthy girl? Easy really—if one couldn't have the things that mattered.

'Can I help you, miss?' the doorman directed politely at the young woman standing hesitatingly on the top flight of carpeted stairs.

'I'm with . . .' Gail gestured foolishly at Kyle Saunderson's broad back and rushed to his side at the reception desk. They stood in strained silence until the desk clerk finished attending to the needs of another guest, and Gail unconsciously fidgeted from foot to foot, out of her element in one of the best hotels in the city.

'I have two rooms reserved in the name of Saunderson,' Kyle Saunderson announced evenly, with no hint of the anger that had preceded.

'Ah, yes, sir.' The desk clerk looked up from the register. 'Mr Saunderson and . . . ?'

The receptionist's enquiring eyes rested on Gail. Kyle Saunderson turned on his heel and for a long moment looked down at the girl by his side, whose wide-eyed gaze shifted nervously about her.

'And friend,' he supplied with sly innuendo.

It was not lost on the other man, nor on Gail who, out of sheer temper, gave way to temptation. The stamp of her small, lightly-shod foot on his seemed to go unnoticed, confirming her growing belief that he was made out of stone, inside and out. Instead he faced the desk again, and with a parody of discretion muttered quietly, 'I hope the rooms are next door to each other.'

Not the flicker of a reaction from the receptionist, save for a bare nod, but Gail fought a silent battle to remove the hand that clamped down on hers the instant the words were out, and was holding her at his side.

By the time they had ascended in the gate-barriered lift Gail had counted to a hundred and still felt like raking her nails down Kyle's cool, mocking countenance, despite the presence of an openly curious porter and bellboy. Only the certainty that she would be the one to lose dignity paralysed her hand.

They arrived at Gail's room first and her active imagination was still devising methods of retaliation, if only they were alone—not realising Kyle's purpose in handing his room key and a generous tip to the porter until he was leaning back on the door that effectively shut out the rest of the world, every bold idea of revenge fled.

'Get out of my room!' she screamed at him, regardless of whether her voice would carry.

His stance became even more casual as he shoved both hands in his jacket pockets. Amused eyes travelled over her body, resting fractionally on the rapid rise and fall of her breasts before moving on to her face, flushed with temper and the embarrassment he had caused her.

'I know,' he said, as if engaging in a guessing game, 'outraged innocent. One of my favourites, and nearly convincing—especially the maidenly blush.' A smile quirked the corners of his mouth at the clenching of small fists, and he began moving away from the door.

'Perhaps you'll find it more convincing when I start screaming!' she threatened, with a mixture of panic and fury, as he backed her as far as the bed.

'Come on, Gail,' he murmured persuasively as she recoiled from the hand stretching out to her. 'You're not scared of me, and you've certainly been alone in a bedroom with a man before. Perhaps even this bedroom?' He used her earlier taunt against her.

'I don't have to take this from you!' she cried out against his ability to make her feel cheap. 'I lived with a married man and maybe that makes me a tramp. But my having your brother's child doesn't give *you* the right to stand in judgment over me!'

Gail had picked angry, fighting words at random, and he spotted the contradiction before she did. 'You said the boy wasn't Barry's.' A hand shot out and trapped her there. 'Remember?'

'I lied.' He wasn't about to give her time to think, as his fingers tightened on her wrist, crushing bone.

'Or you're lying now,' he bit out. 'Which is it?'

Why did it matter to him whether the boy was his nephew or not? From the way he had talked of Barry, family ties were not important to him. Gail shrugged dismissively.

'Which version would you prefer?' she parried, refusing to struggle to release her hand, despite the pain he was inflicting. 'Keep hurting', she prayed silently, 'keep giving me the strength to meet you head-on'.

'You could keep a Freudian psychologist busy for a year with your multiple personalities, Miss Mackenzie,' he mocked her show of toughness. 'From tempestuous woman to wronged innocent to . . . What role are we playing now? Perhaps you'd better give me a cast list, or better still a scenario of the plot.'

Every incisive word accused her of self-dramatisation, and she hated it.

'The plot is: once upon a time there was a handsome, witty, charming prince called Barry Saunderson. And there was a silly, naïve little fool, just off the peat bogs, who fell in love with his smile. And contrary to the laws of arithmetic, one and one made three.' Neither the flippancy nor her defiant expression were quite sufficient to mask the hurting, and Gail gave away more, much more than she had intended.

Kyle freed her wrist, but his hooded eyes still raked her face, piercing through the tough outer shell to the wounds she had unwittingly exposed to his view.

'And still loves him,' he affirmed quietly as she sank on to the bed and tried to hide the tears slipping down her face.

She went rigid at the touch of a gentle hand on her

shoulder, hastily removed, and with every last scrap of her dignity, she managed to choke out, 'Please leave me alone.'

'Silly little fool,' he repeated, soft with a pity that made it difficult to hold back the choking sobs that rose in her throat. But she did. And when the door clicked shut, she stretched out on the bed and turned her head into the pillow that would muffle the suddenness of her tears.

Tears fell for the few glorious months she had shared with a man she had never learned how to other than love; she cried for the beautiful bastard boy, born out of love and in despair; and then, selfishly, for the loss of the numbing detachment that had enabled her to survive, and was being torn from her, bit by bit, by Kyle Saunderson.

And when those tears had ended she lay on her back, trying to understand why this was happening to her, tracing over each incident since that meeting just twenty-four hours ago. She admitted she had done her share of goading and sniping, but no one could reasonably expect her to sit back and meekly take it all when, from the outset, or as near as it made no difference, *he* had treated her like an untouchable. She had turned the other cheek to her granny's outbursts, to Rory's unrelenting condemnation, but this was a time to stand up and fight back—or go under.

'I won't let him make me cry again,' she promised herself, biting her lip to stop another threatening tear. She had to stop hiding, take charge of her life.

She rummaged in her bag for a tattered letter and picked up the telephone. More than likely Peter no longer had a job to offer her, but Gail felt the need to hear a friendly voice.

A waiter told her to hold the line and minutes ticked by before she heard a soft lowlands accent, saying, 'Mason speaking.'

Gail cleared her throat, but that was as far as she got

before she was gripped by a silly fear that maybe the whole world had gone off her.

'Who is that, please?' Peter Mason was impatient to return to the evening preparations.

'It's Gail,' she jerked out, and felt a rush of relief at the loud exclamation of pleasure vibrating through her earpiece.

'Gail, love, it's great to hear from you! I got your letter, at least one page of it, outlining the joys of life on the farm,' he mildly scolded her inadequate excuse for turning down his offer.

'I'm sorry, Peter, I . . .'

'Hey, I was only teasing!' Peter had picked up the strain in her voice. 'Gail, are you OK? Where are you? Off the island?'

'I'm fine,' Gail responded, increasing her pitch so she sounded it. 'And I'm in Edinburgh.'

'You've left the wild and woolly west—that's good news, love.'

Peter shared Kyle Saunderson's opinion—the barrenness of the island was suitable for sheep and not much else; apart from meeting Gail, his short holiday on it had not been a success. 'You're not going back, are you?'

'No, Auntie,' she laughed without resentment. Two minutes on the telephone and Peter was dispensing advice! It was familiar and it felt good.

'Cheeky kid,' he bantered back. 'So what gives?'

She heard someone calling to him in the background. 'Nothing. I just wanted to phone you. You're busy. I'll ring later—some time.'

'Whoa!' he cut into her rambling. 'I can't wait another six months to hear what's happening to you, sweetheart, and they can cope without me. This isn't a one-man operation, you know.'

'Do I detect a faint note of pride?' Gail quizzed, and joined in his laughter.

'Talking of notes, have you sung any lately?'

It was her opening and she chickened out. She hadn't practised in over two years. She couldn't take a job from him, even if he had one to offer. 'What's the new place like? Is it bigger?'

Gail listened to him enthusing over his new venture with an amusing mixture of modesty and pride, relaxed now she had got him off the subject of her life. She didn't want to risk an explosion over the telephone by telling him about Saunderson or the will. He hadn't liked Barry. 'Too old, too experienced, and not good enough,' had been his frank criticism.

'Gail, have I sent you to sleep?'

'No, of course not,' she denied, and sensing he was waiting for an answer to a question she had missed, she admitted ruefully, 'I was distracted for a second, that's all.'

'I asked when you could start? At the club?' Peter repeated, showing he knew full well she had rung for a reason. 'That offer's still open, although you may not deserve it, after keeping me waiting so long.'

'I don't—I mean I can't.' He was making it easy for her, but the doubts came flooding in. 'I haven't done any singing, not since I left the club.'

'Look, Gail, I'd take you on if you were tone deaf,' he assured her, and quickly stifled her protest with a more businesslike approach. 'At present I have a temporary female vocalist who makes it a point of honour to throw an artistic tantrum every night. She looks haggard, to put it politely, and *she* is *definitely* tone-deaf. You'd be doing myself and my customers a big favour if you just stood on the stage and didn't sing at all . . .'

Five minutes later Peter rang off, leaving Gail feeling steamrollered and committed to starting in three weeks. But she had gained some of his enthusiasm and a little of his overwhelming confidence.

The guitar was badly out of tune, with one of its strings actually snapped; it would have been easy to blame Kyle Saunderson's rough handling, but in all fairness it had been a long time since the instrument had been out of its case and cared for properly. A meal, presumably ordered on her behalf by Kyle, arrived while she was fitting a string and was left virtually untouched by an absorbed Gail.

Gradually the chords came back to her, and formed into once favourite melodies, not forgotten but stored in some unused corner of her mind. And the joy of making music returned, like rediscovering one of her senses. She sang softly until a growing ache in the back of her throat forced her to stop, but the feeling of contentment lasted until she slipped into a deep, dreamless sleep.

Suffocated by the unusual warmth, she woke slowly and felt for her wristwatch on the bedside table. Ten o'clock! It just couldn't be. The lateness of the hour dispelled much of her lethargy, as she surfaced out of the tangle of bed sheets.

Barefoot on the luxurious shag pile carpet, she shuffled to the adjoining bathroom, still slightly dizzy with sleep. She'd have to be quick. Surely Kyle had already breakfasted and would be waiting for her downstairs, impatiently cursing her tardiness and reaffirming his low opinion of women in general, and her in particular. It was irrelevant that she had been up before dawn most of her life. So much for her resolve to avoid conflict!

The shower, adjusted to tepid, washed the sticky warmth from her tired body, and she hurriedly dressed in dark blue cords and a bright yellow polo-neck sweater, both of which had seen better days, and she was surprised into worrying about Kyle's critical reaction. She turned from her contemplation of the too-thin figure reflected in the full-length wardrobe mirror, disgusted with her momentary lapse into caring what he thought. It wasn't her fault the bag containing her more feminine clothes had been stolen on her journey home. Anyway, she suspected that she could be dressed like a fashion model and he still would see her as something the cat brought in!

Snapping shut her repacked suitcase, she reassured herself that two more days, perhaps three at the outside, and she would be rid of Kyle Saunderson's disturbing (no, obnoxious, she hastily qualified) company. She had a job to go to and a flat, if Peter was as good as his word. A new life, and this time she wouldn't ruin her chances of making it a successful one. No more highs, no more lows, but she would steer a steady cautious course.

How exasperating! She stood, a case in each hand, keyed up to restart their journey, only to be informed by the receptionist that Mr Saunderson had gone out at eight, leaving instructions for her to be left undisturbed until late morning. And she received her own set of orders in the form of a sealed envelope.

She accepted the desk clerk's suggestion that he would look after her bags while she took morning coffee and biscuits in the lounge. She sat in a corner of the large public room, beside a window, and gazed interestedly about her. In a calmer frame of mind, she appreciated the old-fashioned atmosphere of the room, which combined elegance with comfort in deeply-padded leather armchairs, backed by handmade antimacassars, and gate-legged tables positioned beside each chair. No low glass coffee tables and ultra-modern, functional furniture for one of the oldest establishments in the Royal borough. It looked as though it had remained unchanged for a century—and, Gail mused, catching the eye of the old gentleman in the next alcove, so did its clientele.

Sipping deliciously creamy coffee, she settled back to read Kyle Saunderson's note, written in a bold, decisive hand. Her assumption proved correct as her eyes flicked over the blunt instructions.

'I have some business to attend to in Edinburgh. Buy something smart and presentable, but he back waiting for me at one sharp.

Kyle Saunderson.'

Her irritation at the tone was nothing compared with her reaction to the crisp new notes that accounted for the envelope's bulk. Five hundred pounds to buy something 'smart and presentable'! Observing, and in all probability misunderstanding the smile of her ancient, tweed-suited gentleman in a gesture of sheer defiance and overwhelming temper, Gail ripped the thin wad of money right down the middle.

The regret for her childish action was sharp, if not instant. What if in his own insensitively arrogant way Kyle was trying to make up for upsetting her so badly the previous evening? What if . . .

'Fairies really do live at the bottom of my garden,' she muttered, her derision this time directed at herself. Realising, from the startled look of her fellow guest, that she had not yet broken the habit of speaking her thoughts aloud, she flushed her embarrassment and promptly stuffed Kyle Saunderson's gift, or whatever it was meant to be, in her jacket pocket.

At the top of the hotel steps she shrugged into her duffle coat and pulled her woollen cap over her ears. She had not the slightest intention of using his money, and he'd just have to put up with her—lumps, scruffy clothes and all. Nevertheless the first thing she had to do was find a stationers.

The day was one of contrasts—bright sunlight but with a touch of frost in the air. The cold, however, was less severe than further north, and as she mingled with the busy Saturday shoppers, Gail began to feel quite warm, putting it down to the pressing crowds and the remnants of her heated anger at being treated like a kept woman.

Sellotape bought, she was reluctant to return to the stuffy hotel. Her head snapped up at the boom from the Castle gun overhead. Another hour to kill.

What had prompted her to trail up through the back streets to the clun?—nostalgia, an attempt to strengthen memories that had lost their sharp clarity. Whatever it had been, it was a bad mistake. Little wonder he believed she had been a nightclub singer, she admitted, as she stared up at the garish façade of the building, with its new name surrounded by multi-coloured bulbs and a picture of its female singer in a dress that left little to the imagination. The new management had brought Soho-style entertainment to the club, striving for an image of excitement and raciness. In the cold light of day, it looked cheap and tawdry—incongruous in the capital city, steeped in Scottish history.

It felt even more peculiar taking the hill to the flat she had briefly shared with Barry; the time lapse since she had last made this climb and the fact that she was empty-handed, made it so. No shopping bag full of groceries; no junk-shop find she would swear had been a bargain while Barry teased her for her gullibility.

Unusually breathless by the time she had climbed the rise, she halted at the corner of the street of four-storied tenement buildings that had become fashionable in the seventies. Recognising the foolish sentimentality behind the pilgrimage, nonetheless she felt compelled to carry on.

What bittersweet pleasure had she expected to derive from coming here, or was she rubbing salt into the old wounds to keep herself alive to the pain? Raising her eyes from the cobbled stones of the road, she sought the window of their—his—flat, and was rocked by the fleeting vision of Barry, framed in the bay window as though he had been waiting for her return. Dazed by the power and sense of reality of her vision, she stepped off the kerb into the path of the taxi that was crawling past.

CHAPTER SIX

'Are you all right?' It took seconds for the taxi driver to jam on his brakes and leap out of his cab. 'I thought I'd missed you completely!'

The fright of her last-minute awareness of the oncoming vehicle had caused Gail to slip on the cobbles, and she gasped out, 'I'm fine. The road—it's icy!'

'You weren't looking where you were going,' he accused the girl who had been inches from ruining his perfect, accident-free record. 'You just walked out in front of me, and if I'd been going any faster . . .'

The rest was cut off by a deep, authoritative voice saying, 'Yes, extremely foolish, I agree. I'll take charge of her now.'

Gail didn't have to raise her head to identify the owner of the suave, censuring words, and yet her head lifted automatically to meet cool grey eyes that gave nothing away as they took in her ignominious position. She remained where she was, her legs still trembling, but her silent gaze blatantly hostile.

'Well, mister, if she belongs to you,' the disgruntled driver added with a distinct note of sympathy, 'you have your hands full, so I'll be off and leave her to you.'

And then, as though she was nothing more than a dead cat lying in the gutter, Kyle Saunderson turned away with the other man, apologising for the inconvenience he had been caused and pressing some notes in his hand. Good humour restored, the taxi driver climbed back into his cab, and skirting round Gail, drove away.

'Are you going to sit there all day?' Kyle Saunderson enquired blandly, once more standing over her.

Ignoring his outstretched hand, Gail struggled to her feet, still badly shaken by her near-accident and his appearance seemingly out of nowhere.

Arrogant, smooth devil in his expensive grey lounge suit and silk shirt, making her feel scruffy and inferior! Ungraciously she slapped away the hand brushing loose grit from her coat front, and shot accusingly at him, 'Have you been following me?'

The curling of his upper lip conveyed that such an activity would be most definitely beneath him.

'If I was following you,' he announced with a cool, irritating reasonableness, 'how could I possibly have been at the flat window watching for the taxi you so dramatically stopped?'

The light dawned extremely late and blindingly clear. Her vision had been no ghost, even if his effect was just as disturbing. A hand tilted up her chin and he read her thoughts as though they were written in black and white on the anguished lines on her forehead.

'You didn't realise it was me, did you?' he surmised quietly, his fingers gently trailing to the curve of her neck.

'No, I . . . I mean yes,' she mumbled, confused by the warmth spreading from his light, caressing touch and his steady appraisal of her flushed cheeks.

Again she had the impression that he was reaching out for some part of her that wanted to believe and accept the compassion in his lightened eyes. But she was frightened by it and broke away from the spell he was casting. Hurrying down the deserted street, she shut her ears to his order to stop. She made ten yards before he was spinning her round, holding her immobile by clamping hard hands down on her thin shoulders.

'Let me go!' She hit out at him with her balled fists, but was frustrated by his dragging her close in a rough, confining embrace.

'Calm down, Gail,' he ordered hoarsely as she continued to push frantically at the wall of his chest, 'I don't want to hurt you.'

It was the worst possible thing he could have said. Gail kicked out wildly, feeling a surge of renewed strength as the toe of her walking shoes hit bone.

But her triumph was shortlived. Regardless of possible witnesses, Kyle hauled her against his right side and half carried her across the cobbled road. When Gail gathered the purpose behind his manhandling of her, she ceased fighting him, but caught at his jacket lapels.

'I won't go up there!' she cried her protest aloud.

At least it arrested his attention, stopped him on the step outside the building which she was so violently against entering. He bowed his head and for long seconds his grey eyes seemed to be penetrating their way to her hidden fears. Her mouth framed the word 'please', but the sound was lost in the tight knot of her throat.

'You've made the pilgrimage, so you can't go away without visiting the shrine,' he pronounced sentence with an unaccountable bitterness, uncannily using her same idiom to describe the compulsion that had brought her here in the first place.

Gripping her elbow tight, he forced her up the three flights of narrow stone steps ahead of him, only releasing her at the door of the flat while he drew the key from his pocket. Her last-ditch effort to avoid the inevitable had her pushed against the outer wall and held by the scruff of her jacket collar until his other hand fitted and turned the key.

He shoved her before him into the hallway, slammed shut the door and finally let her go. Gail leaned drunkenly against the inner wall of the hall, fighting off waves of dizziness. Her mind protested, 'No further'. Already the familiarity of the light blue walls and the reproduction prints, set askew by the banging of the door, was tightening her stomach muscles with an absolute tearing panic.

'Please, I don't want to be here,' she was begging, and hating him for forcing her to do it.

'You've been here for four years,' he replied obscurely, pulling her away from the support of the wall and through into the living room.

'Look at your shrine,' he commanded harshly.

On every flat surface—framed photographs. Of her laughing face; of her features in a mask of seriousness caught off guard by Barry's obsession with taking her picture; and of both of them, taken by a newspaper friend, capturing the essence of their loving. His mocking 'shrine' hit her full force as her legs threatened to give way and she collapsed into the nearest chair. And still he didn't let up.

'Doesn't it justify all that fierce, stubborn love you've been nursing all these years?' Kyle jeered, his hand sweeping the room.

But his taunt reminded her, not of the love, but the piercing misery of her last day in this flat . . .

The doctor had been positive about the cause of her sickness and spells of dizziness, and disapproving as his gaze slid over her ringless fingers, but her joy at the idea of a life growing inside her had not been diminished by his cold stare or the warning that she might have a difficult pregnancy. Sure that Barry must welcome it, as she did, and shutting out any murmurings of practicality, Gail had almost run up the hill from the surgery, only a new-born caution for her health slowing her steps to a fast walking pace.

Up half the night waiting for the results of a prolonged conference held by the Secretary of State, Barry had still been in bed when she returned. He had teased her for the bright glow on her cheeks and the happiness shimmering in her clear blue eyes, comparing her laughingly with a child who had just discovered there really was a Father Christmas. Sitting at his side on the covers of the bed and hugging her knowledge to herself for a little longer, that was exactly how Gail had felt. And then she had told him, quietly, proudly, that she was going to have his baby. What had she expected—an initially shocked reaction giving way to a joy that would match her own? But there had only been horror in Barry's agonised eyes, horror that grew as each silent second passed. His confession when it came, barely audible in his shame, was short and killed all the joy within her. His simple, 'I'm married,' resounded in her head, with a deafening clarity . . . Consciousness returned, but the eyes that anxiously raked her face were of a different, darker shade, confusing past and present.

'Why didn't you tell me?' she mumbled through trembling, dry lips, accusation in her tone, but love still clutching at her heart.

'Tell you what?' he urged, brushing the tumbled hair from her flushed cheekbones.

Her vision cleared as the faintness receded and she vaguely shook her head.

Gentle fingers smoothed her brow. 'You're very hot. Do you feel sick?'

'Sick?' she repeated hazily.

'Do you want to lie down?' he asked.

She focused on the man on one knee in front of her chair—unmistakably *Kyle* Saunderson. 'No, I'm all right. It's hot and I passed out for a moment.'

If he himself found the unheated flat quite the reverse, he refrained from saying so. 'I'll make you some tea, or coffee if you prefer.'

'Tea,' she confirmed her need for a restoring drink, and inwardly, for some breathing space.

Resting her head back on the softness of the armchair, Gail closed her eyes until the sound of footsteps on the wood-tiled kitchen floor told her Kyle was no longer in the room.

Save for the disconcerting, embarrassing profusion of

photographs, everything was exactly how it had been left. The same oatmeal tweed suite, still stylish; the bright, modern prints complemented by their background of hessian weave; shelf upon shelf of books, many of which they had bought together. No changes—nothing new, nothing removed—as though time had stood still . . .

An hour, it had taken to gather her possessions together, removing only the things she had first brought with her to the flat, and all the time Barry pleading with her not to go. But the dream had been shattered and she stood firm against him. 'If you loved me, you'd stay,' he had cried at her, but the ugly shame had consumed every other emotion.

After that, Gail had seen him once more. He had come to the club in her fifth month of pregnancy. It had been one of her last working days, for the loose smocks no longer concealed the signs of motherhood, and having caught sight of him in the audience, she had tailed off mid-song, unable to continue. Sitting rigid in the wooden chair at her dressing-room table, she had listened out the promises to seek a divorce from the wife he had ceased loving a long time ago, to send money to her and the child until they could be together permanently. It was an old familiar story, and she had felt cheapened by its retelling. It had seemed then that her love for him had died, unable to survive life's harsh glare when her rose-coloured spectacles had been smashed into tiny splinters. Stone-faced, she had told him she never wanted to see him again. And she hadn't—only love, or the memory of it, didn't die that easily . . .

'Here. I made it strong and sweet.' Kyle's return was abrupt and soundless.

The cup rattled noisily on its saucer and he took it from her nervous fingers, placing it on the telephone table beside her chair. Later Gail was unable to recall who had made the first move, but suddenly she was in his arms, clinging to him as though he was a lifeline with his potent air of reassurance and his hard-muscled strength, and the clean, male smell of him. And when his arms tightened round her, she burrowed into his shoulder.

'Pretend I am someone else if you like,' he whispered throatily, his lips moving against her temple line.

She tensed in the circle of his arms, every nerve in her body immediately rejecting his. Knocked off balance by reliving another time, she had sought and found comfort from the man who was moulding her slight frame to his, but there had been no confusion of identity. His fantastic offer acted like a slap on the face, shocking her with its reminder that it was the wrong brother whom she had wanted to keep holding her tight, suffusing her with his positive vitality.

Sensing withdrawal in the perfect stillness of her body, Kyle went from her. What was happening to her that she allowed this man past the barriers erected so long ago, the foundations of which had been laid in this very flat?

'I'm sorry,' he said.

'For what?' she asked, her voice unsteady.

'Dragging you up here. It was a damn stupid mistake on my part.'

'I came here under my own steam.' Gail surprised herself by excusing his ruthlessness, not understanding what he meant by mistake.

'Why?'

A simple enquiry, but she had no easy answer. To raise ghosts, or to try to lay them finally to rest? She didn't know herself.

'Why are you doing this to me?' she avoided his question with one of her own. 'Backing me into corners, pushing me . . .'

'Is that how you see it?' Kyle matched her quiet

restraint, but his facial muscles had tensed at her accusation. 'Why should I want to do that?'

'Is it the money?' Gail prompted, suspicious that he was playing with her but wanting to end the war of nerves with them. 'Barry's half of the business? You've told me it's worth a lot of money. And money is obviously important to you, but it isn't to me. That isn't meant to sound lofty and high-principled, it's just the truth. I'm not suddenly going to go back on my word and keep the inheritance, so you can stop intimidating me!' Her lilting voice had risen considerably as she rushed towards the end of her speech, and the arms folded across his expanse of chest spoke of his forbearance while he heard her out. Her eyes returned to his face and interpreting the smile pulling at the corners of his well-shaped mouth as smug self-satisfaction, she scowled back at him.

'If I was trying to intimidate you, Gail Mackenzie,' he commented on her sullen look, 'I don't appear to have been too successful.'

But there were more forms of intimidation than angry threats and physical manhandling, and the indulgent inflection with which he pronounced her full name increased her confusion.

He drew closer, his gaze compelling her not to look away from him as he said persuasively, 'And I definitely wasn't. Believe me, Gail.'

'You must take me for a fool, Mr Saunderson!' she attempted to put distance between them by using his surname. 'You treat me like a tramp off the streets, force me to come up here so you can torment me further—and you have the gall to expect me to kiss and make up!' An unfortunate choice of phrase that made her blush to the roots of her hair. His under the breath muttering of 'God, give me strength!' did nothing to improve her mood, although she suspected she was not meant to catch it, as he had briefly turned away.

When he addressed her again, it was with an exertion of self-control.

'Listen, Gail, I may have said some unnecessarily cruel remarks, but you don't make things easy for a man.' And she wasn't making it any easier now, regarding him with uncompromising hostility. He tried again to get through to her. 'I didn't want to hurt you by taking you up here. I thought, perhaps wrongly, that it might be good for you to face up to the past.'

Gail laughed with marked bitterness, hardening her heart to him and his careless patronage. 'I don't need anybody's help, least of all yours!' To his steady, penetrating gaze, she shuttered her face into a mask of indifference.

His reply was soft, as if he was treading on thin ice. 'You can't shut out everybody for the rest of your life, Gail. A person can't survive like that.'

He was wrong. She could and she would. 'Your concern for my mental welfare is both unwelcome and unnecessary,' she said tightly.

'All that toughness is just so much camouflage,' Kyle pursued relentlessly, throwing himself down on the chair nearest hers. 'Do you want to know how I see you, after a little more than a day in your company?'

'No, I don't,' she denied, striving to maintain her aloofness, her eyes fastened rigidly on the oatmeal carpet.

He sighed exasperatedly, 'A little girl who wasn't allowed to grow up properly before life knocked her flying, and who consequently understands so very little about life, or feeling, or men.'

Prepared for abuse, Gail was sent reeling by the quietly-spoken analysis. Her eyes flew to his face, made no sense of the expression that smoothed out the usually grim features, and skated away to inadvertently fix on one of the photographic portraits. It was that other girl he was describing—the one whose head was thrown back in laughter and whose eyes were fever-bright with happiness; she was the one who hadn't understood that what seemed too good to be true really was so.

'You have the wrong girl,' she declared falteringly.

'Have I? My brother carved you up pretty badly, didn't he?' Kyle covered the small, cold hand that lay on the armrest, and Gail steeled herself not to draw away, not to show he was reaching her on any level. 'My sweet, lovable, selfish brother took you and used you, and you were too young to even know the ground rules of being the other woman.'

'I didn't . . .' she bit off her rash disclaimer, but his narrowed eyes told her he could fill in the rest for himself.

'*That* was what he didn't tell you before,' he muttered to himself, recalling the question she had uttered in the first hazy seconds of coming out of her faint. 'Don't you see, Gail, that makes it worse—that he didn't even tell you he wasn't able to marry you?'

'I didn't ask.' She was attacking Kyle Saunderson for putting her through this damaging inquisition, not defending his dead brother. In truth she had assumed Barry's 'for evers' were just another way of saying, 'I want to marry you some day'. She jerked her hand away and rejected his pity with another defensive lie. 'And it wouldn't have mattered if I'd known. I loved him—that was enough.'

He rose abruptly and moved away from her, stopping in front of the bookcase. He seemed to be staring at one of the photographs of Barry and her, and this was confirmed by his slamming it face down on the shelf. When he turned towards her once more, there was no trace of the man who had offered his compassion to her, and for a second Gail wished she had gripped the helping hand he had been holding out to her. But his biting sarcasm immediately obliterated the crazy thought.

'"Love is blind"—trite but evidently true,' he muttered disparagingly. 'Thank God he wasn't able to compound the whole sorry mess by marrying you!'

'Another saying you may have heard—"it's better to have loved and lost than never to have loved at all",' she retorted, smarting from his brutal dismissal.

'What makes you so sure I have missed out?'

'Have I offended you?' she asked, shamming regret and sensing from his return to arrogance she had hit an exposed nerve. 'I'm positive, with your assets, women are more than ready to drop at your feet, begging for your attentions!' She didn't mean character assets, and her tone conveyed her message perfectly.

'All *my* relationships have, at least, been based on honesty,' Kyle growled.

'Meaning?' she flashed back, rising to her feet.

'Forget it.' He shoved clenched hands deep into his trouser pockets. 'I don't think you'd be able to take it, and I don't feel like chasing you half across the city when you start running again.'

'I don't intend *running* away. A walking pace will suffice,' she said icily, and turned to go.

His mock-polite question halted her at the door. 'Haven't you forgotten something, Miss Mackenzie?'

'No, I don't think so.'

'You owe me five hundred pounds,' he said with an attitude of a man pronouncing sentence.

Shocked disbelief had Gail wheeling round. Every arrogant inch of him supported what she had caught in his tone. He actually imagined he had bought her, had tied her to him with his money! Speechless with temper, she threw the envelope down on the floor at his feet, closely followed by the roll of Sellotape, and banged her way out of the flat without waiting to witness his reaction.

She had stalked half the length of Ferry Road, driven on by a mindless, triumphant fury, when another dizzy spell forced her to lean against the glass of the bus shelter. What in heaven's name was wrong with her? She remembered she hadn't eaten properly in days and latched on to it as the reason for the dizziness.

The fury had gone, giving way to considerations of common sense. Digging deep into her pockets, she counted exactly seven pounds and sixty-eight pence. Well, that wouldn't get her to London, or even back to the island. Sure she had started out with more, she concluded it must be in her suitcase.

Half fearful that Kyle would be waiting for her in the hotel foyer, she took an inordinately long time to return.

'Could I have my cases, please?' She was relieved to find the same receptionist on duty.

'Mr Saunderson has collected them for you, miss, and is waiting in the car park at the rear of the hotel.'

Gail had been conclusively checkmated. Kyle had her clothes, her guitar and the rest of her money, the little savings she had left from working. A step ahead of her, he hadn't needed to chase after her.

In spite of the increasingly curious glances of the young man at the desk she sat for a long time on an armchair in the lobby, pretending to herself that she was making up her mind, yet knowing in reality she had no choice. The anger had not left her, but had hardened into an icy resolve to make Kyle bitterly regret his high-handed, autocratic behaviour.

She climbed into the low-slung Ferrari, but did not immediately shut the door. 'I'll make you very sorry you forced me into coming with you!'

When he eventually spoke, he sounded resigned, more weary than angry. 'I already am. Close your door.'

They travelled from Edinburgh to the Midlands without speaking. While Kyle concentrated on making their journey as short as possible, crossing central Scotland to join the M6 at Carlisle and then eating up the motorway miles with the powerful motor, Gail channelled her mind to take an interest in the scenery.

The Lowlands did not possess the dramatic beauty of the West, and one section of roadway began to seem very much like any other. When they reached the Lake District, darkness had fallen, and after an initial thrill of moving at an incredibly high speed in the fast lane, she discovered the monotony of motorway travel that had her several times on the verge of breaking the awful brooding silence.

Only, even if her pride would have allowed her to, she was unable to think of one topic of conversation that was guaranteed to be both neutral and of possible interest to the man at her side. All they had in common was Barry, and Kyle Saunderson seemed to be contemptuous of his brother, while she was . . . what? She wasn't sure any more, and she didn't want to dwell on it.

Silence prevailed until just past Birmingham, when they pulled into a service area to refill the petrol tank. Gail wanted to ask how many more miles before they reached their destination but one glance at his tall, straight figure striding back from the payment kiosk told her to forget the question. Hundreds of miles they had travelled together, and he still looked as intractable as when they had left the Scottish capital. But somewhere along the road Gail had developed some sense of remorse. It was Kyle who had made her go up to the flat—he had probed into her private life, coerced her into making this journey—and yet here *she* was, feeling acutely, absurdly guilty.

Changing his mind about driving straight out, Kyle circled back to the car park.

'I'm going to eat,' he announced without looking in her direction.

He was halfway to the restaurant building when he turned back, making for the passenger door, and yanked it open, nearly causing her to topple out of the car.

'Come on.'

'I'm not hungry,' she said in a small voice she scarcely recognised as her own. Good manners had dictated his return, but there was nothing remotely polite about his tone.

With an abruptness that left her breathless, he pulled her up out of the seat, and resting her against the bonnet, locked the door. She had to run to keep up with his long strides as he propelled her along beside him, but when her painfully-stiff legs forced her to protest, he actually shortened his step to suit hers. When, however, they reached the restaurant, Gail dug her heels in at the entrance.

'What the hell's wrong now?' he asked impatiently, dark eyes raking her worried face.

'Trust you to find a place with waitress service!' His pained expression said 'so what'. Gail admitted sullenly, 'I can't afford to eat here.'

'Owe it to me,' he curtly dismissed her awkwardness.

He was back to treating her like a recalcitrant child and she hated it. 'So you can remind me at an opportune moment that I'm in your debt?' she countered rashly.

'Get in that door,' he gritted out, 'or so help me, I'll leave you stranded here!'

He meant it. She did as she was told.

Gail managed the clear chicken soup, but after a few mouthfuls of the main course he had ordered for her, she was muttering a hasty excuse me before making a dash for the ladies' room. The solid food had threatened to choke her, but she wasn't actually sick, but terrifyingly groggy. She was burning up, and the splashing of cold water on her heated face did little to cool it. The fit of coughing she had been subconsciously suppressing in the car scarred her raw throat, sending shooting pains across her chest. All the signs were there—the dry ache, the feeling of being stifled by an oppressive heat—but she prayed she could fight it off for a few more days.

Calmer, but with her face still flushed, she made her way carefully back to the table. Her food was cold, but she no longer wanted it. Sensing Kyle's scrutiny, she mumbled, 'Car-sick.'

'Do you want to drive for a while?'

His response threw her even further off balance. 'Your car?' she answered, her amazement making her stupid.

'I wasn't thinking of hiring another,' he muttered dryly, a slight smile taking some of the sting from his words. 'One doesn't get sick if one's driving. You can drive, can't you?'

'You'd let me drive your Ferrari?' she quizzed, frank disbelief making her stare round-eyed at him.

'It's only another car.'

'I know that,' she defended, but was genuinely surprised he was prepared to trust her with what must be a very expensive model. 'Are you tired?'

'Not particularly. I'm not exactly in my dotage,' he added with something approaching amusement.

'I didn't mean that,' she denied quickly. There was grey at his temples and fine lines radiated from the corners of his eyes, but his vitality was pronounced, even after many hours at the wheel. He returned her steady, curious appraisal, and when she next spoke it was to the white tablecloth.

'I don't think I want to drive, but thank you very much for offering.'

'Polite child,' he mocked.

Their eyes met once more. 'Why do you refer to me as a child, Mr Saunderson? I'm twenty three next birthday.'

'Perhaps it's the respectful way you address me,' he suggested wryly and then in a more serious tone, continued, 'Or maybe because it's safer.'

Gail didn't understand the quiet statement, but refrained from asking for an explanation. His anger had dissipated over the meal, and detecting his change of mood, she swiftly told him she was going back to the car.

Signalling the waitress, Kyle asked her to wait until he had paid the bill. With careful deliberation, he sorted through his cash until he succeeded in placing the matching halves of one of the torn notes on the platter. Gail's mortification equalled the waitress's gaping surprise, but Kyle seemed to be enjoying both, as his lazy smile moved from Gail to the young girl who had served them. His impact on the latter was noticeable in her blushing response as she picked up the money and the bill, and in her immediate near-collision with a waiter. On her return with the change, her glance at Gail was one of pure envy, and the Scottish girl saw the man sitting opposite her through the young waitress's eyes—handsome, virile, charming. Gail was glad she knew better than to be affected by the surface impression.

'I hadn't time to use the Sellotape,' he explained, laughter lurking in indulgent grey eyes.

'I'm sorry,' she said automatically, then wondered what she was apologising for.

'What for?'

'I'm not sure,' she admitted, and laughed, albeit nervously.

'I was beginning to wonder if you knew how to,' he commented softly.

Laugh or apologise? Well, she wasn't about to ask him which. In this mood, it was difficult to remember to dislike him. When she risked another glance at him she was conscious of being the object of that measuring look that usually preceded some statement or question that she wasn't going to like.

'Hadn't we better go? It's getting late,' she gabbled without any idea of the actual time.

'Gail, there's something I should tell you before we go any further,' said Kyle with less of his normal self-assurance.

'About Barry?' she said huskily, her suspicion growing that the information he was about to impart was not pleasant.

'In a way, yes,' he confirmed.

'I . . . I've got a headache,' she stammered out an excuse that was quickly becoming fact. 'Couldn't it keep?'

Whether he saw it as the cowardice it was, or simply took it at face value, Kyle himself seemed relieved and quite prepared to forgo the matter for the present.

'OK. I'll tell you later.'

Rising, he drew back her chair, and his hand rested lightly at her elbow as they walked back to the car.

A combination of traffic accidents caused by a night fog and roadworks on the M1 saw to it that it was well after midnight when they did eventually arrive at his home, and Gail was so sleepy and hot the last lap of her journey was a blur of hedgerows and woodland. Kyle shook her gently awake, but she was too drowsy to take in much, as he guided her up stone steps and caught her when she stumbled. Too tired to protest or even care, she curved her head under his chin as he carried her up a wide, sweeping staircase, and drifted back to sleep.

CHAPTER SEVEN

Why did it have to be Sunday? To be a wholly unwelcome guest was bad enough, but today was a family day and her presence must be an even greater embarrassment to him.

Sitting gingerly on the edge of the lace-covered bed, Gail wondered whether to remain in the bedroom until summoned or go down of her own accord. Better stay, she thought. In fact she would be distinctly relieved if she was left on her own for the rest of the day; she felt exhausted and incapable of putting on a brave, confident show. At three in the morning she had been woken by a spasm of raucous coughing and the irritation in her throat caused her to drift in and out of sleep through the early hours. It had taken all her energy to dress, and her head was heavy and hot.

Carefully she lay back on the bed and surveyed the room. The best description for the elegant, spacious room Kyle had given her was feminine—completely and utterly feminine in its pink and white colouring, its delicate fabrics and the ornately carved cream furniture. And it was beautiful, she admitted, everything matching and toning in colour, but its very perfection made her nervous. The soft, fluffy wool carpet looked too white and spotless for her to dare to walk on. The idea of hanging her scant collection of clothes in the massive, marble-effect wardrobe seemed like an intrusion.

'Another word,' she muttered to herself. 'I could never have fitted in here.' But Barry had never intended she should. The day she had moved in, he had started making plans. To purchase the lease on the flat. To find a post on one of the Scottish dailies. He managed to do both within weeks, and that had strengthened her belief in their future together. And neither had been particularly forthcoming about their family backgrounds, as though nothing of any consequence had happened before their meeting.

For Gail, seventeen and in love for the first time, nothing had. Was it her inexperience that had attracted Barry to her? She remembered his bland, smiling response to her efforts to become more sophisticated, more, she had thought, of a woman for him and the feeling that his indulgence had actually masked a disapproval of her trying to grow up quickly so the difference in their ages wouldn't matter. 'I want you to infect me with your youth, not the other way round,' he had laughed when he found her in front of a mirror studiously copying the make-up of a model in a magazine which he had promptly tossed out the window. And then he had taken her to the fair to prove that a girl who squealed with delight at her first ride in a dodgem car was definitely not ready for black mascara and purple lipstick.

What had she known about or expected from adult loving? Living as she had with only one parent, her imaginings had been vague and formless. Barry's reverential lovemaking had been like being wrapped in a warm, safe cocoon and she had been grateful for his understanding gentleness. Only sometimes she had lain awake while his even breathing told her he slept, and guiltily tried to quieten the restless murmurings of her body that there must be something more. She had believed that lovemaking would make her a woman, but inside she had felt little different from the girl she had been on the island.

Voices from below interrupted her disturbing reflections and she pushed herself up from the bed. She crossed to the long, double-fronted window—and actually did a double take. Scarcely conscious of her surroundings the previous night, she was totally unprepared for the view that widened her eyes in fright. The window led out on to a stone balcony, and she stood, transfixed by the magnificence of rolling lawns, sweeping down to a sizeable lake, graced at that moment by a family of swans. On the far side there was woodland, stretching back from the water farther than the eye could see. She turned her head to the left and then back to the right, counting the other stone parapets that jutted from the front of the house. Gail knew very little about architecture, but she knew the house was very old, incredibly large and most definitely in the 'stately home' category; she groaned inwardly when she recalled her jibe about 'manor houses' and 'gracious living'. Leaning over her balcony, she realised her bedroom stood directly above the stone-canopied entrance. The voices became clearer as she heard the crunch of footsteps on the forecourt gravel, and instinctively she backed away from the front of the balcony.

It was difficult to recognise Kyle Saunderson in the jean-clad figure strolling down to the grassland, with one child clinging to his neck and babbling with childish enthusiasm for his return, and another, older boy walking by his side. The toddler's excited shout of, 'Daddy, show us the kite in the air!' reached her, and Gail watched, fascinated, as the man she had once considered cold and dispassionate to the core unwrapped the box held by the dark-headed youngster, and drew out a brightly-coloured triangle that was soon fluttering in the wind. She felt a sharp, agonising envy for something that would always be out of her reach, and the knowledge she had cheated herself out of it only served to increase the pain.

Suddenly aware of being observed, she pulled quickly back through the open window. It was going to be even worse than she had suspected. What could Kyle's wife think about his arriving home with a complete stranger? Or perhaps he had telephoned to explain the situation, and Gail's cheeks stained red at the thought. When she recalled her accusation that Kyle Saunderson knew nothing about loving, her embarrassment grew. Seeing him surrounded by his evidently adoring family, she felt it was small wonder he saw her relationship with his brother as sordid and shallow in its impermanence.

His knock was more a warning than a request to enter, for he was standing in the centre of the room before she had gathered her wits sufficiently to answer. Their eyes clashed momentarily and she quickly blanked off all emotion as she sensed his searching gaze on her flushed face. She sat on the edge of her bed and stared down at the fluffy carpet.

'Did you sleep well?' Kyle enquired.

Trust him to play the perfect host; when he wasn't in one of his icy furies, his manners were impeccable, but it did not endear him to her—quite the reverse, in that it smacked of hypocrisy. 'Yes,' she croaked, trying her voice for the first time that day and finding it difficult to force the word out through a raw, hurting throat.

'You were so dead to the world last night, I had to carry you upstairs.'

Damn him for reminding her of her need for his strength to make it up to this room! His hands slipping off her shoes and warm, woolly socks had brought her sufficiently awake to reject any further assistance to undress, and with amused laughter at her near-panic, he had left her alone. She wished he would go away now.

Instead he shortened the gap between them, and said restrainedly, 'You appear to be taking your discovery very calmly.'

Gail stole a quick glance at him through the sweep of her long lashes.

'Why shouldn't I be calm?' If he thought her concerned to discover he was married, he was about to be disillusioned.

'For six hundred miles I've been trying to find the right words to tell you. Despite everything you said to the contrary, I really did believe you cared. I suppose one can convince oneself of anything, if one wants to enough.' Remarkably his derision appeared to be directed towards himself.

'Why should I care?' she threw back at him, affecting a carelessness that was at variance with her initial, shocked reaction at discovering him married. 'It doesn't have anything to do with me.'

'Cold, heartless bitch!' he gritted out, hands clenched at his side.

She was rocked by the sudden, bitter attack, and her voice lost some of its huskiness as she retorted, 'The fact that you're married doesn't bother me, and if you think . . .'

'Married?' It was his turn to look incredulous. 'What in the world are you talking about? I'm not married!'

'But I saw . . .' The protest died on her lips, and she stifled a momentary, unaccountable pulse of relief as her mind raced ahead to its own damning conclusions. Pure, unadulterated rage was uppermost as she cried, 'You have the sheer, unmitigated gall to make me feel like a tramp, to sit in judgement over myself and your brother, when you have a yard full of dirty washing yourself! You are the most contemptible . . .' The string of insults were choked off by the rasping coughs that left her gasping for air.

'Lost for words?' he bit out. 'Attack is only a good tactic if you've got the weapons to use, and I'd like to hear about my supposed dirty linen.'

'Have you conveniently forgotten your bastard child?' she mimicked the cruel taunt he had used on their first meeting, and knowing she had succeeded in disconcerting him, pressed on, 'I heard him calling you Daddy—the little boy out there on the grass. No doubt in your exalted circle, you see yourselves as above the rules that apply to ordinary mortals!'

Kyle cut into her tirade, the throbbing muscle at his temple an indication that he too was struggling to contain a terrible anger her words had aroused.

'I suggest you stop now before we both say things we'll regret later,' he ordered with an unnerving quietness.

Ignoring all the warning signals, Gail continued recklessly, 'It must be nice to be so rich that you're unaffected by public censure! But to me, Kyle Saunderson, you're just as low as . . .'

She wasn't allowed to finish her stream of abuse before he was dragging her to the window and throwing it wide, pushing her out once more to the balcony. In answer to her frantic resistance, he caught her hands behind her back and held her trapped against the stone wall. 'Remember, you started this,' he said hoarsely, before shouting loudly across the forecourt, 'Simon, come here!'

While the boy strolled from the grass to below their window, his command was but a whisper in her ear. 'Take a good look.'

'Yes, Uncle Kyle?' The youngster looked up at him enquiringly, his eyes shifting to the woman at his uncle's side with unabashed curiosity, but it was not satisfied, as Kyle Saunderson simply instructed, 'Get Joel and come in for your elevenses.'

Simon delayed long enough for his interested gaze to rest once more on Gail, and then turned to obey his uncle.

'Barry's son—Simon,' he explained.

'I know.' The boy was about eleven, and although like his uncle, his features were even more pronouncedly similar to Barry's. Had those intelligent eyes merely been expressing interest or was the accusation she had seen in their grey depths real? Gail began to shiver, despite the film of perspiration that glistened on her forehead, and she twisted her head round to him, saying as evenly as she could manage, 'It's cold out here. I want to go inside.'

'Not yet.' He released her hands, and instead placed his

fingers on her shoulders and guided her round to face ahead once more. 'There's somebody I want you to see.'

The older boy was urging the toddler to come inside, and when the latter gave way, with marked reluctance, he tucked the kite under one arm and pulled the younger boy along.

Kyle's voice in her ear, low and throaty, seemed to become part of her own thought processes as the two children grew nearer and nearer.

'Not my bastard, Gail. Hair the colour of sunset gold, that refuses to lie in anything but wavy disorder. A chin with just a hint of the cleft to come, and as stubbornly determined as his nature. No, not my beautiful baby boy,' he denied, no longer with any harshness, and his firm hands moulding her shoulder bones as if he was trying to infuse her with his strength.

The truth lay in his soft commentary, and in the face of a four-year-old boy that was her own in perfect miniature. It shattered barriers of self-preservation and brought every part of her alive to the pain and wonder of it until the chaos that was her brain threatened to break apart. And she surrendered herself to the escape of merciful oblivion.

CHAPTER EIGHT

Gail's first instant of consciousness was dominated by the bittersweet vision of the boy who was her son but not hers in any other way, and then a dark head, looming above hers and blocking out every emotion but a tearing pain that ripped through her prone body. She heard a voice that seemed to be coming from outside, screaming out her agony, and her head throbbed with its piercing loudness until she fitfully pressed herself into soft, feather-down pillows to shut out the frenzied cry. But it grew inexorably louder and she thrashed her head frantically from side to side. Barely conscious of anything else, she offered no resistance as cool hands on her burning flesh rolled the jersey up her thin arm.

Mercifully the noise, more animal than human in its high-pitched intensity, receded, and with it the pain, until it was a dim, almost imperceptible ache that had no substance. She felt herself slipping back into a state of total numbness, her lips forming a smile of gratitude for her release . . .

Her throat was achingly dry and there was a heavy weight pressing down on her chest. Running a tongue over parched lips, she attempted to speak to the woman who sat knitting in a chair next to her bed. Did she know this woman? Yes, in dreams that gave the impression of reality until they became clouded over by the blanket of fog swirling round her brain. Was she a nurse? She wore a linen uniform of some kind, but less formal than that of a hospital nurse.

'Awake at last, dear?' The smile was friendly and reassuring, and she tried to answer, but her head was full of cotton wool. 'Would you like a drink of something?'

Gail managed a nod. She tried to sit up in the bed, but she had no strength to support her body, and sank back on the pillows, exhausted by the effort.

'A nice strong cup of tea.' The older woman propped her up on the pillows, and held the cup to her mouth, gently pouring the warm liquid down her throat at a pace her state of drowsiness could cope with. 'My name's Mrs Macbeth and I work for Mr Saunderson,' she explained, straightening out the crumpled bedclothes with a professional deftness.

Gail wished she could ask the standard, 'Why am I here?' or suchlike, but it came back to her all too clearly. Her eyes shifted nervously around the room, and Mrs Macbeth answered her unspoken question. 'Mr Saunderson had you moved nearer his room in case you called out in the night,' she said, with a distinctive lowland Scots accent, diluted by years spent away from her native country, and then ran on, 'I have a flat above the garage and he refused to let me sit up with you.'

Memories of a damp cloth cooling her forehead and a soothing, masculine voice—real or imaginary? 'How many . . .' she tailed off as the words stuck in her throat.

'Five nights, and running a temperature high enough to make us thank the Lord for antibiotics. And Mr Kyle acting like a . . .'

Gail was not to hear how Kyle Saunderson had reacted to having her ill on his hands, because a small boy stood framed in the doorway, nervously twisting and turning the knob. 'Joel needs a biscuit.'

'Joel needs a good spanking, if you ask me,' Mrs Macbeth responded laughingly. Crossing from the bedside, she scooped up the youngster with an energy that belied her sixty-odd years.

The steady, silent stream of tears coursing down her patient's face stopped Mrs Macbeth midway between door and bed. The mute appeal in the girl's eyes was unmistakable, and perceiving the frightened, cornered look, she whisked the protesting toddler out of the room with promises of satisfying a growing appetite.

It was all too much and too soon. With a witless panic she had responded to the child's presence, and she gratefully swallowed the sleeping pill offered by Mrs Macbeth on her return.

It was dark when she next woke. Stronger than when she had last surfaced, she managed to pull herself together up in the bed. The heat was oppressive. With a drowsy singlemindedness, she craved fresh air. Her legs scarcely seemed part of her, but they took her out on the balcony where she sank breathlessly down on a wicker chair in its corner. A cool breeze fanned her cheeks, beginning to clear her head of the effects of the sedatives. She'd move back inside the moment she became cold, but for now she eagerly drank in the night air. Everything was so still and peaceful, except for the vaguest rattling of the door.

For a second he stared at her—fragile and childlike in white cotton—in frank disbelief. Idiotic girl! He delayed long enough to pull on some pyjama trousers.

'What the devil do you think you're doing?' he rapped out, tense and angry, crossing from his half of the balcony.

The chill of the spring night and his sudden appearance sent Gail's teeth chattering. Kyle was wrapping her in his towelling robe, still warm from his body and smelling of male talc, and she had no choice but to clutch on to his shoulders, as he scooped her out of the chair and carried her effortlessly back inside. It was Gail whose heartbeat quickened alarmingly as her fingers spread against his hair-coarsened chest. He laid his burden gently down on the bed, but when he would have straightened away from her, she instinctively tightened her grip. His eyes were questioning, and she uncurled her fingers and dropped her arms to the bed. Illness left in its wake a desire for comfort and she was embarrassed by the weakness she had shown.

Kyle tucked the bedclothes round her and briefly left her, returning with a thermos flask. He was not wearing the top of his pyjamas but had not bothered to close it, and Gail swerved her gaze away from the black, curling hair that covered his smooth-muscled chest. She plucked nervously at the bedcover while he poured hot, sweet tea into the flask top. He held it to her mouth, cradling her head with his other hand, and she drank deeply and thirstily until he eased her back on the pillows.

'Warm?' he asked crisply, pulling the covers higher.

Gail nodded, not trusting her voice. She felt no resentment against his authoritative manner, for his efficient tending to her needs seemed strangely but distinctly familiar.

'Do you feel up to talking?' he enquired, sitting at the edge of her bed.

Gail, fully awake, was acutely averse to being left on her own, despite the certainty that his consideration wouldn't last the course of any conversation between them.

'Yes, if you like,' she agreed with an unaccustomed meekness.

'Only if you're strong enough. You've been ill with a fever that looked at one point as if it would develop into pneumonia. In your undernourished state that probably would have wiped you out,' he told her with a matter-of-factness that was wounding. 'You don't act like someone who's grateful to find herself alive.'

'I needed some fresh air,' she defended huskily, and immediately relented with, 'I'm sorry. It was a stupid thing to do.'

'Why didn't you tell me you were sick?' he demanded will ill-concealed impatience, and anticipating her denial, added, 'Dr Tanner said you must have been burning up for at least a day.'

He made her sound like an irresponsible child! 'I thought it was with anger,' she lied, and flashed him a look of pure defiance.

'You should learn to control that quick Celtic temper of yours.'

'It's only . . .' Gail was loath to carry on. Telling Kyle he was the one person who got under her skin sufficiently to arouse her usually even temperament was like telling him he was someone special.

'We do seem to strike sparks off each other,' he concurred with her unfinished protest. 'Why do you think that's so?'

It was a serious question and she answered it in the same vein, choosing her words carefully. 'Partly because of the circumstances that brought us into contact, but owing to our widely different . . . backgrounds, it's not likely that we'd ever have been friends anyway.'

Her search for an appropriately neutral word was not missed by him, and he commented, 'I believe you're what's commonly termed an inverted snob, Gail Mackenzie. And I don't particularly want to be your *friend*.'

'And I definitely don't want to be yours,' Gail avowed tautly, holding out against the attractive smile that slanted his firm-lipped mouth.

'Good, that leaves us a range of much more interesting relationships to choose from.' The insinuating tone and the teasing light in dark grey eyes had her shifting nervously in the bed. 'You look ready for flight again, only I don't think you'd get very far this time. Do you?'

'Get off my bed!' Gail immediately wished the hasty order unsaid, but it had been an involuntary response to the impression that his closeness was penning her in.

'Why?' he queried mildly.

'Has no one ever told you that it's unhygienic to sit on

the patient's bed?' she snapped out the first excuse that came into her head.

'Mm. I preferred you when you were ill—all sweet and clinging and utterly feminine,' Kyle drawled, making no sign of moving.

'I don't believe you.'

'"Kyle, don't leave me",' he purred in a faultless imitation of her lilting accent.

'You're lying,' she countered, lacking a note of total conviction. Had she, in the frightened depths of fever, begged for his attention?

'Maybe,' he conceded in a smug tone that made her even more uncertain. Lightly laying his hand on top of hers, he offered, 'Truce?'

'Or unconditional surrender?' she returned with immediate disbelief.

'If you like,' he replied, and laughingly supplied, 'I surrender—unconditionally. You do take prisoners, I hope.'

What was he trying to achieve?—if it was to unnerve and confuse with his easy charm, he was succeeding.

'Why did you do it?' she blurted out. 'Why did you bring my . . . the boy down here? To torment me?'

Kyle shook his head and said with heavy patience, 'Not the villain of the piece this time, Gail.'

'Barry,' she muttered to herself. She couldn't think clearly. The pieces didn't fit. 'When?'

'Joel was about a week old when Barry brought him home.'

The fleeting, painful vision of a toddler laughing excitedly at a multi-coloured kite flying up to the clouds prompted her next wondering question. 'Why does he call you Daddy?'

'My brother was still living with his wife, publicly at least. He deposited the boy with me. I was the one around when Joel started talking,' he explained evenly.

'If he thinks so, then everybody else must . . .' Gail grasped the implications of what he was saying, and the rest was swallowed up by a mixture of guilt and shame.

Kyle gently tilted her head up, smoothing away the fall of hair that hid her expression. 'Gail?'

'I'm sorry,' she breathed, unable to hold his enquiring gaze. As an apology, it was hopelessly inadequate. 'The mess I've made of everything . . .'

'Listen to me, Gail,' he spoke firmly, stilling the hand clutching at the bedcover. 'If you're feeling sorry for me, your sympathy is totally wasted and definitely unwelcome. And Joel—well, he's happy and healthy, and apart from a stubborn streak, the source of which is no longer a mystery,' his lips quirked with amusement, taking any bite from the remark, 'he possesses a nature as bright as the mop of red hair on his head.'

'Gold,' Gail corrected automatically, and for the first time they laughed together. But Gail's laughter was short and nervous, her mouth quickly straightening and her brow furrowing with anxiety.

'To see it all as a mess from beginning to end is like denying the boy's right to exist,' he instructed, his tone gently persuasive. 'You understand?'

Gail understood well enough. It was the same sort of reasoning that forced her to cling to the fact her son had at least been a love child in the true sense.

'You called it a sorry mess,' she recalled without re-crimination, but threaded with the hurt he had inflicted.

'You have a most unfeminine characteristic of storing away all the unpleasant things said to you,' Kyle groaned aloud, squeezing her hand in almost playful punishment, 'but I suggest we begin again. This time, on the right foot.'

Confused blue eyes lifted, disputing his sincerity, but he met them steadily. And again Gail had the absurd impression he was reaching out. 'Too close.'

'Gail?'

'Nothing,' she mumbled. The caution had not been meant for him.

Sensing her withdrawal, Kyle rose from the bed, but he lingered for a moment on her trembling lips and the blinking of her eyelids. She was on the verge of tears, but wasn't ready to cry in front of him. Not yet. 'We'll talk some more tomorrow. Get some sleep, and stop worrying,' he ordered with mock sternness, switching off the bedside lamp.

Gail wanted to say so many things, but all she could manage out of the turmoil was, 'You're very kind.'

The touch of his lips, featherlight and cool, was almost imperceptible, but his parting echoed in the darkness.

'No, not kind, Gail.'

Softly spoken, it nevertheless held a nuance of warning, the exact meaning of which eluded her as the door clicked shut behind him.

Every assumption she had made about Kyle Saunderson's character and motives had been turned on its head. No wonder he had raged against her pretence of indifference for the boy he had adopted as his son! And if he no longer saw her as flagrantly immoral, it was no thanks to her determined efforts to foster such an impression.

Kyle was right; she understood so very little about life or her own feelings for a man who could make her shake with rage against his arrogance and then tremble with fear under his incredibly gentle handling.

Eventually she slept, exhausted by an attempt to come to terms with a past, her view of which was dramatically shifting, and a future filled with uncertainty.

CHAPTER NINE

'Eat a bit more, lassie,' Mrs Macbeth urged, glancing up from her knitting just as Gail was pushing her half-eaten breakfast away from her. 'Help you get your strength back.'

The old woman's crisp but kindly meant order had Gail picking up a slice of toast and chewing a corner, even though she had no appetite.

Mrs Macbeth's smiling approval was motherly and prompted Gail to ask, 'Is your family in Scotland, Mrs Macbeth?'

'Well, I have a sister in Argyllshire, but that wouldn't be what you are meaning. All the family I want are down here—Simon and Joel, and of course himself, His Lordship.'

The description of Kyle Saunderson brought a smile to Gail's lips, but it was quickly followed by a sharp prick of conscience. Still, it wasn't easy to lose one's prejudices overnight. 'How long have you been here?' she asked.

'Nigh on forty years. I came down with Mrs Saunderson.' Gail's curiosity was roused, but she resisted the temptation to probe further. It seemed, however, Mrs Macbeth was more than happy to chatter on. 'She was like yourself—pretty and very young. Met the old Lord, Kyle's father, when he was up for the August shoot.'

'Lord?' Gail gasped.

Mrs Macbeth dropped the knitting on her lap and looked as perturbed as the younger girl. 'He's not told you, lassie, and here's me running on, my foolish tongue getting the better of my common sense! And he'll be in one of his black furies when he finds out. Still, least said, soonest mended,' she mumbled distractedly.

'Kyle—he's a lord?' Gail was desperately hoping she had misunderstood.

'Well, yes and no—inherited the title on his father's death, but he winna use it. Canna bear all that fawning, or so he says. But I still think on him as the Lord, being his father's heir.' She frowned again. 'You'll no tell him I told you, for it'll put him in one of his moods?'

Unimpressed by the idea of a title, Gail nevertheless withered when she recalled her comments on the English aristocracy. No wonder Kyle had been amused by her hasty disdain of marrying a lord! Wonderingly she asked, 'Are you scared of him too?'

'Mercy, no! I've known him since he was a bairn. But he's got some of his father's temper, although none of his unrelenting pride, and when he's calmed down again, he's as sweet and apologetic as his dear mother.' Gail struggled to imagine Kyle Saunderson suiting the adjective sweet, and failed. 'You'll be seeing that side one day, lass.'

'Has Kyle explained who I am?' Gail couldn't accept any more of the woman's kindness under false pretences.

Mrs Macbeth picked up her discarded knitting, and with the needles clicking busily, she replied evenly, 'No, but my eyesight is as good as ever it was, and one look at your bonnie face . . .'

No condemnation in the tone, but Gail, in all fairness, couldn't leave it like that. 'Kyle and I, we aren't . . . weren't . . .' Acute embarrassment blocked the rest of the stuttered explanation.

'Dinna take on so, lass. After their mother left, I almost brought the two of them up, and I'm no one to jump to conclusions. Not like others round these parts.'

Gail stared sightlessly at the counterpane. What a mess, and it was all her fault!

The warmth was back in Mrs Macbeth's voice as she

went on, 'My anger's no against you, lass, but the so-called friendly neighbours—they delight in scandal more than ordinary folk, like you and me.'

'Please don't.' The woman's understanding made Gail feel worse. 'I don't deserve it—if you knew . . .'

'My poor little lamb! I know well enough, for surely I helped to spoil young master Barry until he took for granted anything he wanted should be his. A dreamer, he was, and his not taking things seriously was his charm, but it proved a weakness when he got older.'

'Where's Simon's mother?' Gail voiced another fear.

'*Happily* married to an American businessman.' Mrs Macbeth stressed the word 'happily', 'but Simon didn't take to the man or the country. Very fond of his uncle, he is.'

'Mrs Macbeth, did . . . did Joel's arrival ruin things for Kyle? Between him and someone special?' Why had she asked that? She didn't really want to risk the answer, unearth more damage done.

'No.' The one-word denial didn't sound very convincing and Mrs Macbeth expanded, 'Oh, he's an attractive man and there's many a one who has fancied herself as Mrs Kyle Saunderson, but he's no time for them—not on a permanent basis, anyway.'

The confirmation of his own professed opinion that women had their limited uses should have pleased her, since it suggested that her son had not had any drastic effect on his personal life. And it did, only she experienced a contrary dissatisfaction as well.

Mrs Macbeth's accent, more heavily pronounced in the company of a fellow Scot, penetrated Gail's musings. 'Of course, he was too young to understand, and it has soured his attitude to women.'

Gail intuitively knew she had missed something important, a key to Kyle Saunderson's complex personality, while her mind had been wandering. But it seemed like prying to ask for a repetition of the information she had missed.

The day passed agonisingly slowly, her solitude interrupted once by a young maid who brought a light lunch and whose silent but almost tangible curiosity left Gail wondering if the whole household would be as shrewd and observant as Mrs Macbeth. Had she imagined the girl's speculative gaze on her red-gold hair and blue, widely-set eyes?

In her depressed state, it was difficult to concentrate on the books and magazines that had been placed on her bedside table. Hearing the voices of laughing children, running along the corridor late in the afternoon, caused her to give up on the novel she had been desultorily reading, and she found herself listening for the small, high-pitched voice that had said, 'I want a biscuit.'

'Not *my* beautiful baby boy,' Kyle had declared. Not hers either, despite the fact she had given him birth. It had been hard, painfully hard, to give him up the first time, but now he had shape and form in her mind's eye it could tear her apart. Only she could see there would be no other choice. And she was scared of being in the same room with him, terrified that in a moment of madness she would stake her utterly false claim. 'Joel, I'm your mother and I want you, always wanted you.' In her mind she could visualise his horrified reaction, but would that stop her acting crazily? At all costs, she had to keep away from him.

She drifted off to sleep after a light supper and woke hours later to find Kyle standing at the end of the bed, watching her.

'How long have you been there?' she mumbled sleepily.

'Not long.' He moved forward and becoming impatient with her struggles to prop herself up against the stack of pillows, he placed firm hands just above her waist and helped lift her up the bed. Her flinching was instinctive but had his mouth tightening with annoyance.

'I forgot you don't like being touched. How long have you had this aversion?' he challenged with heavy irony.

Gail's first thought was 'nothing's changed', and she put the question that had been bothering her all day. 'Joel? How did Barry get custody of him?' It came out abrupt and hostile. So much for good intentions and he was answering her before she had a chance to do anything about it.

'When we were in Edinburgh I checked with your uncle,' he told her with a tone that was degrees more reasonable than hers. 'A combination of money and Barry's rights as father of the child ensured his co-operation. The hospital thought your uncle was looking after the baby till you were better, and you were probably ignorant of normal adoption procedures.'

Gail remembered her uncle Sandy's assurances that the baby would be found a stable, loving home while she lay, exhausted by the difficult birth and racked by doubts of whether she was doing the right thing. She had cried all the way home to her bedsit after the Sister of the maternity ward had asked her, on leaving, if she was looking forward to seeing her baby. At the time she had believed the busy nurse had made a painful but understandable mistake. She knew her uncle Sandy was fond of money, but was nevertheless bitterly shocked by his duplicity. And she found no consolation in her own ignorance over never once considering the absence of legal adoption papers. Kyle Saunderson's touching of her hand brought her back to the present.

'Don't be too hard on yourself, Gail,' he soothed, accurately reading her thoughts. 'Your uncle told me you were too ill to know what was going on around you.'

Gail believed she couldn't be *too* hard on herself. In her weakness she had helped create a child who would have to bear the stigma of illegitimacy for the rest of his life, when she of all people knew exactly what that entailed. Even her attempt to undo that wrong and have the boy adopted had failed because she had lacked the courage to see it through herself.

'Why did Barry do it?' The obvious answer that Barry had wanted his child didn't fit the circumstances; he seemed to have left the care of the boy largely to his brother.

Kyle took off his jacket and drew a long white envelope out of the top pocket, before slinging it over the back of the bedside chair.

'I found this, addressed to you, in Barry's papers.' He sat down heavily in the chair, but made no move to give it to her.

And Gail, strangely, was not eager to have it. Barry's importance to her life was receding, as though images and memories of him no longer had any place in her present.

'I don't think I want it,' she said shakily.

'Why not?' His tone gave the impression that her answer was important.

But all she could choke out was, 'I'm not sure.'

'Scared its contents will threaten your schoolgirl fantasies in some way?'

The derisive comment had her snatching the envelope from his loose grasp and ripping wide the seal. She read,

My darling girl,
      Impossible to express what you meant to me. In the face of our child I see the sweet loveliness that is you and in my mind I cherish every loving moment we spent together. When I was free, I wanted to come back to you, only I lacked the courage to risk it. And now I have left it too late.

The money is yours if you want it, but my real legacy is our son. I have kept him safe for you until you were older and ready for the responsibility. I remember your momentary joy at the knowledge of his existence—the joy I killed.

Pray God this brings it back,

Barry

Grand, empty gesture! Initial numb disbelief gave way to the impulse to rip the letter into two, and she would have repeated the action had not the pieces been wrested from her fingers.

'May I read it?' Kyle took her silence for assent and rapidly scanned the lines and then re-read them with more careful attention.

'Quixotic but sincere,' he stated dryly, 'and he obviously knew you better than I gave him credit for.'

In the absence of its actual target, her pulsing anger directed itself against Kyle. 'So you think I'm capable to turning up out of the blue, accepting a fortune and trying to take away a child from the only home he's ever known!' she spat at him before twisting away in the bedclothes.

'I didn't mean that,' he denied calmly, and then, frustration rising at her rigid, unresponsive back, ordered, 'Turn round and face me, or so help me I'll . . .'

He didn't have time to finish the threat before Gail confronted him once more, flaming with a temper that staved off the hot, stinging tears gathering at the backs of her eyelids. 'You'll what? I'm not frightened of your anger, Kyle Saunderson!'

'No, you haven't even got the sense to be that,' he uttered deprecatingly. 'And if you don't want me to forget you've been ill, I suggest you wipe that sulky expression off your lovely face.'

Convinced that his 'lovely' was a mocking echo of Barry's tribute to her looks, she responded starchily, 'I was not sulking! I've never sulked in my life.'

His crossing to the dressing table and picking up a

pearl-backed hand-mirror were totally unexpected, and she was facing her own reflection before she realised what he was up to. Even the cursory glance at her features showed a full, colourless mouth forming a provocative pout.

'I don't see it,' she lied, casting her eyes quickly down, 'but then I don't spend an inordinate amount of time staring into mirrors.'

'It shows,' he threw back at her, while replacing the mirror on the dressing table.

Insulting boor she thought, as he reinforced the fact that her hair was in wild disarray and her face, devoid of make-up, had a sickly pallor apart from two bright, angry patches of red on her dimpled cheekbones.

'You really are determined not to arouse the interest of any member of the male sex, with your drab clothes and churlish behaviour. Once bitten, twice shy?' he speculated with the lift of one black eyebrow.

He was back to delving into her personal life, and she didn't like it one bit. 'You forget Rory,' she recklessly pointed out her supposed involvement with her cousin.

'I didn't say you achieved your objective. You had a stranglehold over your cousin all right, till he was gnawing his guts out for the wanting of you.'

'That's a disgusting lie!' she stormed back, forgetting any desire to create the wrong impression. 'I never did anything to encourage him.'

'I never said you did,' he countered, his apparent calmness underlining her own virulent reaction. 'But no man gets as angry as your cousin was about another man on the scene out of brotherly love. I should imagine that your air of young, untouched innocence was the only thing that saved you from being thrown flat on your back in one of the sheds.'

If he had been in a rage, his very crude remarks would almost have been forgivable, but said in that dry, conversational tone they were too much for Gail. They banished all thoughts of maintaining the uneasy truce that had briefly existed.

'You've got it all wrong, Kyle Saunderson, and I was beginning to think you infallible! Rory had no need to *throw* me on my back, as you so graphically put it.' Insufferable man, he was actually smiling at her bold insinuation, as though he saw right through her.

'Harking back to those halcyon days in the hayloft,' he laughed outright. 'Little fraud, you automatically blush at the merest mention of anything sexual.'

With his cutting assessment of her small, slight body and his implication that she was sexually repressed, or even worse, frigid, he was stripping her of any claim to womanhood.

'You seem to be forgetting the sort of relationship I had with your brother,' she retaliated, knowing how distasteful this proud aristocrat found his brother's attachment to her. Sure by the lines etched around his mouth that she had scored off him, she prayed he would drop the subject.

'Impossible to forget, with Joel as a constant reminder,' he responded, with what sounded absurdly like regret. He caught and held her hurt gaze and his tone dropped appreciably lower. 'But difficult to believe that those blue child's eyes have ever been glazed with passion from a man's lovemaking. Did my brother treat his darling child like precious Dresden china? Was he scared to make a woman of you?'

His eyes seemed to be penetrating to her most hidden layer, exposing secret doubts and dissatisfactions she had once felt. Her rash, stupid tongue had got her into this, but she couldn't handle it any more—this truth game Kyle was playing with her.

'I don't want to talk about it,' she forced out.

But he ignored her protest as though it had never been voiced. 'Because he wanted a little girl, desperate to give her love to someone, be thankful and adoring for his attention, not a mature woman who might not find it enough to just be a perfect, undemanding toy.'

'Shut up!' she screamed, her hands frantically covering her ears to shut out the cruel, cynical analysis. 'He loved me, he loved me,' she chanted as a protection against the destruction he was wreaking.

Strong fingers threaded through her hair, dragging her hands away and then holding her face rigid so that she was compelled into awareness of the dark head suspended above hers and of every cruel phrase he uttered.

'He was obsessed by you—your youth and your innocence. It must have torn him apart, the conflict between the honest, dishonourable desire to make love to you and the need to keep you a sweet, trusting child who wouldn't recognise his weaknesses. But somehow he managed to do both. It's a pity there wasn't time for you to grow up and grow out of him.'

'You don't understand.' He was mixing her up terribly, making it near impossible for her to think straight. 'It wasn't like that.' She shook her head, half in denial, and half in an attempt to loosen his grip.

'Tell me what it was like—being a pregnant teenager, lying in a hospital bed, no man to bring you flowers and no baby to . . .'

'Stop it!' she sobbed. Why was he doing this to her, bringing out all the submerged pain? 'He would have come, but he wasn't free.'

'Don't look away,' Kyle ordered harshly, brutally forcing her head up once more. 'That didn't stop him taking you.'

'—He loved me.' The tears rolled soundlessly down her cheeks.

'And he knew you well enough not to risk you turning him down. And you would have, wouldn't you?' he stated uncompromisingly.

'You'd stay if you loved me', Barry had declared. At the time, Gail had been too horrified by the discovery that he was a married man to do more than react, to clear out of the flat. But she had left his letters unanswered and eventually unread, and when they had been replaced by the cheques she had sent them back, until she realised that Barry needed to keep giving them to her, even if she didn't use them. And never once had she considered going back—not under any conditions.

'Yes,' she gulped, but it didn't satisfy Kyle as his fingers pressed harder into her throbbing temple. 'Yes, damn you, yes! Yes, I would have turned him down. Is that what you want to hear?'

Indeed her forced, angry confession seemed to have finally exorcised the devil that had driven him on, and there was tenderness replacing all the savagery in him as his fingertips slowly traced the outline of her features, wiping away the tracks of her tears. 'It's a beginning.'

'No, I don't want to talk about it again, ever!' she cried anguishedly, and his reply, when it came, was low and hypnotic, as soothing as the caress of his open palm on her cheek.

'All right, we'll do it your way. I don't want to hurt you any more. We'll forget I ever had a brother and we'll start from there.'

'I can't,' Gail choked out, not even sure what he was asking from her. 'It's too late.'

His hands travelled downwards, feathering over her skin until they rested on her shoulders. 'No, just in time, Gail. You've been frozen in limbo between child and womanhood, and now's the time to cross over.'

The firm touch of his hands, their pressure gradually increasing, imbued her with a strength that tilted her head back in defiance of him. 'I am a woman already.'

'Prove it to me,' he challenged softly.

And Gail knew then what he expected—it lay in the

silent message transmitted by grey eyes that had lost their hardness and the slightly-parted lips of his mouth hovering over hers.

Nerves made her run the tip of her tongue over her dry lips, but it caused him to sharply draw in a breath. And yet he waited for her move, her proof that she was a woman. He stayed motionless as she slowly inched towards his mouth and placed her sweet, damp lips on the firm coolness of his in a kiss that was as short as it was chaste. Her eyes flew open to witness his reaction and she was not surprised at the expression of light mockery that confronted her. She had meant to kiss him properly, to act out the charade with a false bravado, but the barest contact had shaken her enough in its impact on her confused senses. Strangely breathless, she forced an excuse for her reticence, her unwillingness to carry on with what must just be a game to him. 'I don't think that . . .'

Kyle cut in with, 'Don't think. Don't talk. Just open your mouth . . .'

And she did, but to rail against his terse instructions, not to receive the full intimacy of his mouth as it pressed her into the pillows until he held her sweetness trapped and defenceless against his probing, searching lips. Panicked by the totally unfamiliar, violating kiss, she started fighting him, grasping handfuls of thick straight hair and desperately trying to pull the rapacious mouth away from hers, but he seemed impervious to the pain. His breathing became more laboured, and she realised her resistance, the pain she was inflicting, only served to excite and make him more determined to reinforce his complete dominance. Now badly frightened, she released her grip and silently screamed a prayer that if she lay stiff and lifeless, he would lose pleasure in making love to a block of wood. Miraculously it seemed to be working as the pressure on her bruised lips eased and her relief caught her off guard and unprepared for the gentleness of his lips as they lingered on hers, persuasive and soothing, wiping away the traces of his earlier brutality. This gentle playing stirred a bittersweet ache that had her fighting once more, only this time the odds were even greater, as the hands that reached up to his shoulder, instead of pushing him away, curved round his neck, under the hair brushing against his shirt collar.

And suddenly the featherlight touch of Kyle's sensuous lips became unbearable—it tantalised and aroused, but left her wanting, needing more. Just as the sound of a low, triumphant murmur deep in his throat didn't stop the urgent movement of her lips as they gave their own response, begging him to satisfy the longing he had created. Still he held back, and shifting her hands to his broad back and sharply digging into the hard flesh that lay under the white linen of his shirt, Gail was ready for his mouth swiftly descending and taking what she was now willingly offering. And they met on equal terms, both simultaneously taking from and giving to the other.

Everything was sensation—pure and simple and beautiful sensation, as one hand slid away from her neck and wandered over the curve of her shoulder, memorising each detail of the burning flesh that trembled against Kyle's palm, until, satisfied that its knowledge was complete, it moved on and down. The borrowed nightdress, several sizes too large, proved no obstacle as he exposed her breast to the seducing trail of his fingers, and Gail could not stifle the moan of her sheer delight as he stroked their hardening peaks. It did not matter any more what they were to each other—strangers, poles apart in every way, warring enemies—she wanted him with a fierceness that swamped all other considerations. No longer confined by the bedclothes that he had pushed away, she arched her body, glorying in the sound of his rasped, uneven breathing as it mingled with hers.

Without warning his mouth left hers, a low agonised

groan escaping his lips as he rolled away from her and off the bed. In disbelief Gail watched him retreating towards the window. Throwing it wide, he drank fresh air into his lungs.

Hot waves of humiliation at his abrupt rejection and shame at her own weakness choked her. She wouldn't have stopped him, couldn't have if she tried, and he must know it; but his contempt for her had, in the end, overridden any other impulse. And the drugging, heady desire died in her, replaced by a consuming anger that hardened her eyes and her heart to him.

'Don't look at me like that,' he pleaded softly, moving back towards the foot of the bed.

'How do you expect me to look—all soft and melting?' she flashed back at him, the hurt making her voice strident.

'I had to stop. You're not well enough yet to . . .'

How dared he pretend that a concern for her health was the reason for his rejection! Well, she knew better—she wasn't good enough for him—too skinny, too plain, just a little nobody. 'Shop-soiled', Kyle had once called her. He wasn't the only one who could pretend, and her face-saving repudiation came from the fierce pride that had so badly deserted her moments before.

'You thought I was going to let you make love to me?—though perhaps that's not a very apt description for the purely mechanical motions you practise!' The thinning of his lips was a warning she chose to ignore. 'I suppose your inflated ego allows you to believe anything, however absurd.'

'Gail, don't do this,' he said quietly. 'There's nothing to be ashamed of.'

His attempt to calm her missed its intention by a mile. 'I'm not ashamed,' she lied. 'It was a game—nothing more. It would be a cold day in hell before I'd have you willingly in my bed!'

'You wanted it, Gail,' he replied, struggling to hold on to his control. 'Your creamy, silk-soft skin was on fire for me and I wanted . . .'

'Oh yes, I was enjoying it while I was able to pretend.' She had to shut him up, to salvage the self-respect he was trying to relentlessly destroy. 'Only my imagination was rapidly failing me.' Gail paused, absorbing his frowning incomprehension, before she delivered the killer blow. 'You're not the man Barry was!'

The pain she had inflicted slashed his strong face and she had to hold out against the treacherous urge to rise from her bed and run to him, to tell him how she really felt—scared and confused by the overpowering effect he had on her senses. But she had pierced his male vanity, nothing more, for the brief vulnerability had changed quickly to an intense fury that had him slamming the door of her bedroom.

'You've won, you fool,' Gail told her other self who was crying into her pillow like a stupid baby. She had pushed Kyle away for space to breathe and think, and now she had regained her splendid isolation. Only Kyle Saunderson had invaded the far corners of her mind and left his mark so that her every thought and feeling was touched by him, coloured vivid by the intensity of his lovemaking. How could she desire such a man till her flesh ached for release, even when she knew he despised her?

She could not love him. Love wasn't like that.

CHAPTER TEN

It was the first good day of the year and unusually warm for April. The sun shone high in a cloudless blue sky. A gentle breeze fanned Gail's face and the pleasant smell of newly-cut grass teased her nostrils. She looked out on the beautiful grounds, past even lawns to the far side of the lake.

For days she had strained to listen to Joel's lively, boyish chatter, waited at her window for him to come running out of the house to play in the spacious grounds. He rarely walked anywhere—life, for the adored child of the house, was too good to be conducted at anything less than full speed. One afternoon Gail had ventured to his bedroom with its slanting roof under the eaves of the great house. From the threshold she had watched his lips moving contentedly in his sleep while his arms wrapped tightly round a shabby teddy bear, the sort of toy that had been in a family for a generation or two. As she was on the verge of coming closer, a noise from the end of the corridor had sent her darting back to her own room, profoundly grateful that the banging of a bedroom door had come to her rescue and snapped her back to her senses.

Joel had slipped behind the boathouse, but any second he would reappear, pedalling frantically on his lap of the circular lake. Yes, there he was, a bolt of reckless speed on a bright blue tricycle, breaking world records on the gravel footpath.

She had been mistaken: he wasn't a toddler any more, but a sturdy little boy, dressed in striped tee-shirt and dark blue shorts, brimming with high spirits that kept his young nursemaid fully occupied. That he liked the pretty teenager was evident in the smiles with which he charmed her; nevertheless Gail had noticed how frequently he contrived to lose this watchdog who spoiled his fun under the adult guise of 'keeping him out of mischief'.

Once round the lake, he gave a victory salute to an imaginary audience, and then, magnanimous in his triumph, waited for the panting girl to catch up with him.

'Did you see that, Betty? Faster than the speed of sound or light, or both even!' Alert blue eyes became aware of his companion's struggle to catch her breath. Slipping his hand into hers, the little boy declared earnestly, 'If you want, you can cycle my bike round the lake this time, and I'll run after you. I don't mind.'

Betty looked from the serious-faced youngster to his miniature three-wheeler and back again, reacting in the only possible way to the absurd, generous offer—with laughter.

'You don't get me that way, young Joel,' she reproved teasingly. 'Afternoon nap time!'

'Oh no!' Joel moaned, trying, but not very hard, to tug his hand away. It was an oft-repeated ritual that would end up with him being tucked between the soft sheets of his bed, gazing up at the sailing ships on his bedroom walls until his eyes shut of their own accord and he drifted into pleasurable dreams of gleaming cutlasses and evil pirates and buried treasure. But it wouldn't do to give in too easily—after all, it wouldn't be manly.

'Oh yes, my lad. If you don't need a nap, I certainly do!' Betty wagged a threatening finger at her reluctant charge.

'Then you can have my nap for me,' Joel reasoned, flashing a bright smile to reinforce his suggestion.

'You think you can charm the birds out of the trees,' she scolded mildly.

'Why should I want to do that?' the boy returned, slightly mystified by the unfamiliar expression. 'You've got it wrong, Betty. It's snakes you charm, not birds. With a pipe. I've seen it in a book. You have a basket and you blow into the stick . . .'

'Never mind,' Betty groaned her interruption of the lesson. 'Bed—and now! Or when your dad gets home, I'll have to tell him you've been naughty,' she had recourse to the threat that was always guaranteed to do the trick, and raced him up to the front steps, letting him win by several yards.

Their lighthearted dispute carried up to the house, and to Gail, who was watching and storing away each detail. She backed away as they drew near and ran up the steps of the house. It would not do for her to attract Joel's attention; even from a distance, the ache to have and hold her son filled her head with crazy notions that shocked her. Now Gail could understand the torment that made women snatch children from prams; that Joel was her child, both physically and legally (for she had signed no papers), didn't make the wild schemes that came into her mind any less wrong.

She should go back into the room, do something about the clothes strewn across her bed, but instead she sat heavily back on the balcony chair. Tomorrow she'd be leaving, but there was time enough to pack her case before the early morning train to London. For now, she wanted to sift through the scene she had just witnessed.

How much had she learned from silently observing the actions of a child? Enough to realise that he was happy, and any move on her part to interfere with his life would be selfish and utterly disastrous—but not enough to know what he was really like. *Did* a child inherit his characteristics from his parents? His looks were hers, with no trace of the dark Saunderson ancestors who lined the upper gallery walls. But how fervently she hoped that his nature would not be tainted by any of the characteristics that made her feel so inadequate. She wanted him to be clever and bold and sure of himself—a Saunderson. Only it wasn't the boy's father she visualised when she made this judgment.

In the end, all her thinking, no matter how hard she tried to control its direction, ran back to Kyle Saunderson. He had been gone for four days, ever since their last stormy interchange, the memory of which made her blush with a mixture of shame and anger. He had left with Simon, whose holiday was over, but he had not returned to the house after driving the boy back to his school in the Midlands. Despite his absence, he dominated the household! Mrs Macbeth's conversation was littered with references to him—so much so that Gail had taken to avoiding her. It was hypocritical to listen to the older woman extolling his virtues, while she herself so violently disagreed. 'For Mrs Macbeth's "strong and generous" read "arrogant and calculating",' Gail thought. Learning that, at twenty, he had been forced to leave university to take over the family business after his father's death only confirmed Gail's view that he would have assumed the responsibility as part of his divine belief in his own superiority.

What Gail found difficult to rationalise was the reason behind his management of Barry's affairs. While Kyle had been at Oxford studying engineering, Barry, just a year younger, had been making the grand tour of the cities of Europe. It was Kyle who had allowed some capital to be invested in a failing newspaper so that an opening could be created for Barry, who had no interest in the family firm. But Mrs Macbeth painted a picture of a man who had loved and tolerated a younger brother who had relied on him to extricate him from the careless situations in which Barry got himself involved. It did not fit with her image of a Kyle Saunderson jealous of his brother's easy charm, but rather the opposite—it suggested a protective pity for a weaker, less stable brother.

So where did that leave her in Saunderson's organised,

disciplined life? Nowhere. She was the last loose end—or perhaps loose woman was more appropriate to the way he had treated her—and he had tied it up in a neat, efficient knot that morning. It had been his sole contact with her since he had left the house—a terse note, brought by his lawyer, instructing her to thoroughly read the documents concerning the disposal of Barry's estate, and to affix her signature only if she was completely satisfied with the arrangements.

There had been no direct request to leave, but she had read between the lines of his bold, decisive handwriting, and even if he did say, 'We'll sort out other matters when I come home in a couple of days,' she knew better. Business had apparently taken him to London, but the city was only an hour away, so there could be just one reason for his continuing absence—her. He wanted her gone. Well, she wasn't going to stay where she wasn't welcome. She had a job to go to, and a good friend in Peter Mason, who would have found her somewhere to live; and she had no need of any help from the lofty lord of this manor to organise *her* life. She was used to coping on her own, wasn't she? She liked being on her own. No ties, no responsibilities, free as a bird . . .'

'Damn you, Kyle Saunderson!' Gail cursed him aloud for all the silly tears she had wept in the past few days, as she tasted another salty drop on her top lip. 'You're not going to make me cry again!'

She knuckled her eyes hard until they were smarting with pain, and toppling the chair in her haste, marched back into her room. With abrupt, angry movements she stuffed the clothes into her battered suitcase, careless of crushing them, and snapped the locks on her disordered packing. If she could just stay mad at Kyle long enough to get out of the oppressive domain, in peace and private she could nurse the wounds—no, bruises—he had inflicted.

Tucking the suitcase to the back of the wardrobe, she left the room and quietly slipped down the stairs. On the way down to the lake, she picked up a companion in the form of the old labrador she had seen wandering the grounds. Her slow pace suited his shambling gait, and he followed her round the lake, goodnaturedly accepting this stranger in his territory.

They made for the boathouse that sat parallel to the lake, with a wooden jetty running along its side. Curiosity had her standing on tiptoe at the window and she made out two canoes stacked on racks against the far wall. The smaller one would be for Simon, and perhaps later, Joel, and underlined how little she could have been able to give her son, if . . . cross with herself, she dismissed the recurring game of 'ifs' in which she was never the winner. Testing the dryness of the jetty, she sat down on the far end and leaned her back against the boathouse.

'You're a trusting slob of a dog,' she murmured affectionately, as her canine friend stretched himself out in the sunlight and laid his head across her legs. He took as his due her rhythmic stroking and promptly fell asleep.

It was getting on for the warmest part of the day and Gail was becoming drowsy in the direct line of the sun, but she was reluctant to disturb the animal who was snoring contentedly in deep sleep. And soon she joined him in slumber, catching up on some of the rest she so badly needed.

An hour slipped by before she blinked her eyes against the glare of the sun and felt the first rush of relief at emerging out of not-so-pleasant dreams. Gail drew up her stiff legs, the weight of the dog's head gone. She dazedly watched the dog's comic progress as it scrabbled across the wooden boards, having lost all signs of its former indolence. The loud, excited barking started up the moment it rounded the corner of the boathouse and continued without interruption as the labrador raced, with more fervour than grace, back round the lake pathway. Gail's surmise of 'rabbits' was immediately cancelled as she shuffled forward to the very edge of the water, and caught sight of the real centre of the dog's attention.

For once she saw him first, standing on the iron bridge that spanned the watershed which allowed water to drain from the lake after heavy rainfall. His summary dismissal of the dog with a brief clap on its back wasn't necessary to transmit his mood over the distance between them. Fury was written in his hands-on-hip stance and the quick sweep he made of the perimeter of the lake. He missed her on the first pass and probably wouldn't have spotted her on the second, if she had not jerked backward at his harsh, vibrating shout of her name. But the sudden, involuntary movement had him homing in on her in seconds.

Leaning back on the boarding of the boathouse, Gail accepted the inevitable as she heard the crunch of running footsteps. He didn't need to run, Gail fumed, she wasn't going anywhere. She concentrated on gathering all her wits for the coming onslaught, when his striding form shook the jetty itself.

Gail refused to acknowledge him, even when she sensed him standing over her, blocking out the sunlight. Just her luck! She would have been gone tomorrow—could have gone today, after seeing his solicitor.

'Mind if I sit down?'

The quietly spoken question differed widely from the expected abuse or contempt, and Gail's head shot up. His jacket, hooked on one finger, was slung over a shoulder, and his sleeves rolled up to expose powerful hair-covered arms, dark against the pristine whiteness of his shirt. Beads of perspiration stood out on his high forehead and he looked—well, not angry, anyway. Gail shrugged.

He joined her against the boathouse, and loosening his tie, he half-turned towards her. 'How are you feeling?'

'Well enough,' she offered stiffly. Well enough to leave,

because that must be what he was asking, behind the concerned note.

Slowly he appraised her, from her riot of red-gold hair freshly washed and trapping glints of bright sunlight, over her white sleeveless tee-shirt and jeans to her small, bare toes curling into the soles of her open sandals. And when he finished his examination he left her skin tingling and warm.

'You look . . . mm, golden. I said a warmer climate would suit you,' he mused. His eyes scrutinised her face again, and alluding to the bright spots on her cheekbones, he added, 'But your colour is a bit too high. Are you sure you're all right?'

How could he expect her to react to his intense, calculating stare, but with embarrassed heat!

'I . . . I fell asleep. In the sun,' Gail mumbled back, and when he frowned disapprovingly, she excused herself with, 'Only for a few moments. It was very warm.'

'I can see that, you have a smattering of freckles,' he told her, briefly touching the bridge of her nose with a finger. 'You must have been asleep when I was calling and you didn't answer . . . unless, of course . . .'

She had been hiding from him, Gail finished for herself. If he was trying to provoke, he was managing it. She ordered herself to keep cool, but his next mild remark broke the resolve almost as soon as it had been made.

'Mrs Macbeth has been telling me how charming and well-behaved you've been!'

It was the well-behaved that did it, as she flashed him a look of cold dislike and rounded on him with, 'Only you know different, don't you?'

'Do I? I wonder,' he replied pensively. 'Will the real Gail Mackenzie please stand up?'

She meant to do just that and walk away from him as quickly as she could, but when she drew her legs up to rise,

Kyle curled his fingers round her upper arm and held her fast.

'Stay!' he barked out the order, and immediately cursed himself under his breath for his curtness. 'I'm sorry, I didn't mean it like that. Please stay, Gail. We need to talk.'

He removed his detaining hand but kept her there with the strain that had suddenly crept into his voice.

'Why should I? I don't want to talk to you.' She wanted to match his reasonableness, but she didn't trust him.

'I've left a conference room full of people, picked up a ticket for speeding on the M4 and probably gained a few more grey hairs on the way,' Kyle groaned with mock frustration, 'and the girl doesn't even want to speak to me!' He tilted his black head to one side and tried and failed to coax a smile from her.

'I . . . I don't believe you,' she stammered nervously, but no longer convinced that his turning up when she was on the verge of leaving was merely coincidental.

He searched in his jacket and pulled out a piece of paper and tossed it into her lap.

'Exhibit number one,' he presented his case, and waited for her to peruse his speeding ticket, before continuing. 'I could give you the second half of the speech I failed to deliver, but I warn you it's very dry and uninteresting. However,' he paused for reflection, 'now we've entered the age of the micro-chip, with its multifarious ramifications . . .'

'Oh, stop being so silly!' Gail interrupted crossly. He was turning her inside out again, as she had known he would. She wished he would stop smiling down at her, with that melting, seducing look in her eyes, playing cruel tricks on her confused senses. 'And stop making fun of me!'

'Gail, Gail . . .' he moaned softly, reprovingly, 'if you just for one minute regard me as something other than public enemy number one, you'd understand I wasn't laughing at *you*. Give it a chance . . . for sixty seconds.' Deadly seriousness had taken the place of humour, as he cast her a long, penetrating look before he drew away and supported his head back against the boarding.

Gail gave it more than the time he had requested as she stared out at the clear, slow-moving water, rippled by the merest whisper of a breeze, and tried to gain insight into a man whose good humour and gentle persuasion were much more potent weapons than any of his black furies, as Mrs Macbeth had dubbed his temper.

Somehow he had learned of her intention to leave. Of course! It was obvious. Mrs Macbeth had probably come up to her room after lunch, seen the suitcase and clothes carelessly dumped on the bed and telephoned him in London. She couldn't have known Gail was waiting till the next morning. But her going surely didn't account for the way Kyle had rushed back here? She had imagined he would greet the news with satisfaction, after slight annoyance at her making her own arrangements.

Oh, but she was incredibly dense sometimes! There could be only one reason for his panic and the relief she had sensed on finding her still on his property—Joel. From her rather secretive behaviour, he had concluded that she wasn't planning to leave on her own. The realisation was like a slap on the face, stinging and humiliating. Stinging because he had actually believed her capable of it; humiliating because if insidious, unwanted thoughts counted, she was guilty as charged.

Her gaze shifted from the lake back to Kyle Saunderson. His eyes were closed, his breathing even, and believing him asleep, her eyes lingered, studying each feature in turn. Devoid of mockery or harshness, his face was undeniably handsome, perhaps because of, rather than despite, the stamp of arrogance in the straight nose and high, angular cheekbones. Most women would find his self-assertive attitude a source of attraction, but she hastily excused herself from the category. He had been right, in theory anyway, in the judgment he had made on her this time, but that didn't make him right, full stop.

'I hope the verdict is favourable.' The complete alertness of grey eyes that were suddenly returning her scrutiny told her he had only been resting and was fully aware of her open appraisal.

It was dishonest of him to let her assume him to be asleep, and she answered snappishly, 'You don't need my opinion, Kyle Saunderson. You were born with a belief in your own superiority, and I'm sure thousands of women have been more than willing to foster it!'

'Well, hundreds,' he laughingly corrected her exaggeration. 'Can I take it from your prim disapproval that you're not about to become one of their number?'

'Crowds have never been my scene,' she replied disparagingly.

'Oh, you wouldn't be just one of the crowd,' he countered, apparently unmoved by her antagonism. 'And clinging, simpering women may feed the ego, but they scarcely entertain a man's mind.'

'But all you want from a woman is . . .' she tailed off, leaving his 'bed and kitchen' relegation of her sex unvoiced.

'A man can change. And no one could accuse you of being simpering or clinging, Gail Mackenzie.' He dropped the hand that had lifted to stroke the hair tumbled on her forehead at her automatic flinching, but the lazy indulgence was still there, in his lightened eyes and the way he gave her her full name. 'Listen, I know we started badly, but I feel . . .'

'I'm leaving—tomorrow. Today, if you prefer. You can drive me down to the station to make sure I get on the train,' she declared in a rush. Well, at last she had wiped that deceptive expression off his face; he looked like a man who had just been kicked by his favourite horse.

'You're not going.'

Not 'I'd like you to stay'. She hadn't, after all, expected it, but neither had she anticipated the adamant opposition.

'I've done what I promised—signed over the inheritance,' Gail added.

'And the boy? What about him?'

'He . . . he makes no difference to my leaving.' She strove for an impersonality that would conceal the bitter longing, and when Kyle pulled her round towards him, allowed him to search her expression for insincerity.

'Your brave little face lies as badly as you do, Gail Mackenzie,' he announced softly.

She struggled to maintain her pose of indifference. 'It may be difficult for an arch-chauvinist to understand, but I don't like children. Ask Mrs Macbeth how much interest I've shown in the boy.'

'I did.'

'Then you know I haven't . . .'

'Gone near Joel,' he completed her proof of detachment with no trace of disgust for her callous behaviour. 'Yes, she told me. Mrs Macbeth has always prided herself on a thorough understanding of human nature, but you have her totally stumped.'

'It's perfectly straightforward. I just don't care.' Gail laboured each word, forcing herself to meet his penetrating look head on.

'Is that really why you've been ignoring him?' he offered a chance to back down. When she nodded her confirmation, his hand moved from her shoulder to grasp her chin so that she was unable to look away as he asked in the same low, gravelly tone, 'Then tell me the reason you've been surreptitiously watching him for days.'

No explanation came to her lips, but it would have been futile anyway, for the truth had been revealed in the anguished closing of her eyes. Presenting a tough uncaring front had enabled her to keep some measure of control, but it crumbled pathetically under his pressure. Her hand rose to brush away the signs of her vulnerability, but Kyle tugged it away, saying, 'Don't be ashamed of crying, Gail. We need to release our emotion in some way, or it will build up and break us apart.'

'Keep your pity and your lordly patronage, Kyle Saunderson,' she gulped back the threatening tears. 'I don't want it and I certainly don't need it!'

His hands slipped away, but he showed no resentment at her rejection. To the back she immediately presented to him, he murmured, 'You have more than your fair share of pride, Gail Mackenzie. And pride can make a lonely bedfellow.'

His purposeful quote brought back memories of her abandoned behaviour on their last meeting, serving as an unpleasant warning of the consequences of losing her identity and self-respect. Brusquely she rubbed the back of her hand over her moist cheeks, ignoring the handkerchief that appeared in front of her, and threw back at him, 'Pride is not the prerogative of the English aristocracy!'

His sigh was heavy with resignation. 'I thought the "lordly" was just sarcasm. Who told you? Iona Macbeth and her chattering tongue,' he surmised accurately. 'I had hoped it wouldn't make any difference to you.'

'If you think it impresses me in the slightest or that you'll have me touching my forelock . . .' she rounded on him, blue eyes glittering with the remnants of unshed tears and a surge of hot anger, welcome for its effective stemming of any further tears.

'Perish the thought,' he interrupted her tirade with the suspicion of enjoyment at her emphatic denial. 'It's not my fault that I was born with a position in an outdated feudal system, to use your words, but I'm being thoroughly damned by you for it!'

The indulgent inflection was back in his tone. Why couldn't she make him mad any more?

'Oh, but you can,' he conceded, making Gail aware she had voiced her confusion, 'only it dissolves the moment I look into your baby-blue frightened eyes.'

CHAPTER ELEVEN

On the way back to the house, Kyle surprised her by asking what she thought of his 'white elephant'. Gail shrugged offhandedly, not about to admit she found it as intimidating as its owner, and he went on to tell her more about the mansion, its architecture and history, in a tone that hinted at family pride but at the same time made it seem more like a home than an imposing showpiece.

That it was indeed a home was underlined by the excited youngster pulling free from his nursemaid and running over the spring grass, almost too quickly for his short legs.

Gail was stabbed by a sharp, hurting jealousy of the man who was holding her fast at his side, but it changed to alarm as the small figure fell over, yards short of them.

'He's all right,' Kyle reassured her. The features so clearly her own hovered on the point of tears and then broke into a wide grin as Joel decided that any slight bump was secondary in importance to reaching his father. Swung high the moment he hurtled into the arms stretched out to him, the little boy screamed with delight at the rough handling, confident that he was safe. As though he sensed the exclusion that must hurt Gail dreadfully, Kyle slipped the boy down to rest on one thigh, and faced her once more. 'Comes from tough stock,' he said with more than a suggestion of admiration. 'Say hello to Gail, young man.'

Gail stood, rigidly holding herself back, inside shaking with fright, but her son showed no reticence; leaning forward, he placed a noisy, enthusiastic kiss on her cheek, before bestowing on her a wide, friendly grin.

'The sick lady is better, Daddy,' he announced happily, unconscious of any tension and quite willing to accept the tentative hand that touched the curls framing his small face.

When she could no longer control the trembling of the hand that wonderingly fingered the soft red-gold hair, Gail dropped it back to her side. Kyle lowered the boy to his feet with the instruction to go and wash his hands and knees before afternoon tea.

'He's so open,' she marvelled, gratitude mirrored in wide, unshielded eyes for the loving treatment that had made him that way.

'He likes kissing pretty ladies.' His laughter teased her ready blush. 'But yes, he's special,' he agreed with a thread of seriousness.

And the thought 'he loves Joel very much' crept into Gail's head, and made her feel pleasure and pain in equal measure.

'Come on, Joel will be waiting for us.'

'I can't!' she cried out, resisting the light pressure of his hand on her arm. Couldn't he see that every minute she was near her son would make the leaving that much more intolerable? Increase the risk of her doing something crazy?

'Trust me, Gail,' he urged, and when the conflict of doubt didn't disappear from the anxious face upturned towards him, he made the choice for her, striding up the steps and pulling her after him until they reached the lounge.

It would have been enough to observe and listen to the small miracle that was her son, but Kyle was determined to involve her in their conversation over tea. He did so with an ease that made her inclusion natural and had Joel directing his bright chatter to a captive audience. And when Joel had finally wormed his way on to her knee, for he was still young enough to appreciate comforting, she caught Kyle's smiling approval over the top of her son's head and it left her floundering with the impression that the control over her own life was slipping away from her. That, in the end, it wouldn't matter what she said or thought or felt about anything.

And he, with disturbing intuition, had read her mind. When Mrs Macbeth left the room with a reluctant Joel, he observed obliquely, 'Scotland lost its independence a long time ago, but that didn't make it any weaker as a nation. You should learn from your history.'

'That's not quite correct,' Gail retaliated immediately. 'The two countries were unified under one *Scottish* king, James the Sixth.'

'Trust you to know something like that! Inevitable, I suppose, with a head full of ballads about wars long past but not forgotten,' he mocked her nationalism, and catching her suspicious glance, continued, 'Your uncle told me you were a folk singer, although I'd already ruled out anything less savoury.'

'Why?' Gail's question was barely audible, and Kyle crossed over the Persian rug to place his lean body next to hers on the brown chesterfield, so close that any movement on her part would mean them touching.

'Night club singer to milkmaid—I couldn't reconcile the two.' He trailed his fingers down her bare arm, observing, 'You're trembling.'

'Perhaps I have a touch of fever,' she lied huskily, the casual caress increasing her physical awareness of him to the point where every nerve was tautly strung against the possibility of his arms closing round her. But the emotion that had sent her quivering was far removed from revulsion.

'Perhaps we both have,' he suggested softly.

His forehead was cool and smooth to the touch as he pressed her palm against his brow in a pretence of seeking her opinion on the state of his health, and her resistance had been minimal when he had made the gesture. It was his hand covering hers that was causing her to explore the contours of his handsome face while he commanded throatily, 'Feel, Gail. Flesh and blood, warm and alive like anyone else.'

She knew she should break away, but she was incapable of fighting the compelling grey eyes that held hers, seducing in their tenderness and binding her to this intimacy. The kiss on her open palm was featherlight and sensuous, part of the spell he was casting. And for a moment she was breathless and airborne, only the triumphant shaping of his firm male mouth sent her crashing back to earth.

'Stop fighting,' he urged, hoarse and muffled against her hair, but when she continued struggling to pull away from him, he allowed her to rise from the sofa.

Gail moved unsteadily to the window and leaned her head against the coolness of glass. Stop fighting, he had said—stop fighting *him*, he meant. Just let him move in and take over—or take and discard? The sight of Joel stumbling after a plastic football rescued her anger, for envy was a crippling emotion.

'You have everything and you still want more,' she cried out in protest when he joined her at the window. Did he want *her* or just to prove he could have his brother's mistress, as well as his child?

And what did she want?—to keep what little she had left of her self-respect, her reason argued, while her body still trembled a different response.

'You could have a share,' Kyle offered quietly, following the direction of her gaze.

'I want none of it.' She emphasised her lack of interest with an over-vehment, 'Keep your grand house and your acres and your . . .'

'I meant Joel,' he interceded disarmingly. 'What do you want for him?'

'What do *I* want for him?' she echoed in disbelief. 'I abandoned him.'

'And that makes you think you have no rights,' he followed her thought processes. 'You didn't want to give him up, did you?'

'No, but I wanted . . .' a smile of encouragement tempted her to continue her impulsive speech, '. . . a home, with two loving parents, where he wouldn't be ashamed of who or what he is.'

'First-hand experience?'

Why the question? He had a file on her and surely knew about her own upbringing. 'I don't want to talk about it.'

'That's your response any time I try to get near you,' he commented with a measure of frustration. 'How about learning to give a little?'

'Are you suggesting I'm a taker?'

'No, and don't get angry again.' His eyes slid briefly to the hand unconsciously clutching at the green velvet of the curtain and Gail snatched it away. 'You do that when you're scared too. You're neither a taker nor a giver—you just don't want to let anyone near enough to hurt you again.'

Gail backed from him fractionally, an involuntary action that was confirmation of what he was saying. 'We were talking about Joel.'

He raked a hand through his thick, straight hair with ill-concealed exasperation at her persistent hostility. 'Before I met you, Gail Mackenzie, I was enjoying a relaxed middle-age!'

How dared he blame her for disrupting *his* life! 'If you think, Mr Kyle Saunderson, that you've brought any improvement to my life, then you're one hundred and one per cent wrong!' Gail railed against the absolute gall of the man. 'You come stampeding through my life with all the arrogance of your aristocratic forebears until I'm not even sure whether I can still tell black from white, right from wrong . . .'

The sudden lazy grin dried up her rush of furious exclamation and made her hand itch to slap the self-composure off his well-cut features.

'I wouldn't, if I were you,' he eyed the flexing of her fingers, mocking her ready temper, 'or I might think you're also having problems distinguishing love from hate and assume your taking a swipe at me is actually an invitation.' He was openly enjoying the effect he was having on her, but before she could tell him how ridiculous his insinuations were, he turned serious again, and said unequivocally, 'On the subject of Joel, there is no way I'd give him up, not now.'

'You think I'd expect that?' she said, more hurt than indignant, her eyes drifting once more to the little boy turning inexpert cartwheels on the grass. What could *she* give him in place of this magnificent home? Nothing but her love and that wasn't enough. He needed protection and stability, and she had none to give. 'You asked me what I wanted all those years ago, but the situation has changed. I want him to stay here. You'll look after him, won't you?'

'Best way I know how,' he promised quietly in response to her wavering appeal, and then more hesitatingly, 'But to have two parents is still the best thing for the boy.'

'That's not possible. Not now.'

'Isn't it? It's up to you.' Gail's deepening frown made it plain she understood neither the aggressive-sounding challenge nor his concentrated speculative look, and, almost a reprimand to her slowness, he clipped out, 'I could get married.'

Sixty seconds ticked by and Gail was still trying to make sense of her own reaction to his statement. Kyle was waiting for her to say something, his mouth a tight line of impatience and his arms folded over his broad chest, but she could hardly cry out her first thought—'I hate the idea'. One thing was for certain, he wasn't asking for her permission, and she didn't want to betray her immediate and total abhorrence which *had* to be rooted in her imagining of another woman as mother to her child. Eventually she managed, 'That's surely up to you.' She had matched his cold tone, but she hadn't been rude. So why was he looking so black and furious?

'Damn it, woman, you aren't waiting for me to go down on one knee?' he growled.

'Down on one knee?' she repeated stupidly, and the meaning of the phrase struck her at last. And if things hadn't been straight in her mind before, they now spiralled off into absurdity. 'Are you . . . are you proposing to me?'

'You,' he barked out, and for once avoided meeting her questioning eyes with the attitude of a man confessing to some heinous crime.

'To me?' Her brain was trying to catch up with the conversation and her tone reflected her amazed disbelief.

'There's no one else in the room,' Kyle returned, biting sarcasm in the face of her incredulity and grasped the crook of her arm, his fingers bruising the flesh as they tightened. 'Will you marry me, Gail Mackenzie?'

For one timeless, tense moment their eyes locked, as they mentally shifted round each other like opponents in a boxing ring. Why was he asking her to be his wife? His scathing reply was proof that he viewed the idea with distaste, but his grim, humourless mouth was telling her it was a perfectly serious proposal.

He seemed to be suffering some awful, crushing torment as he rasped out, 'A simple one-word answer will do.'

Aware of his meaning, Gail could nonetheless only gasp, 'Why?'

'I don't suppose you'd believe I want to marry you

because . . . because I'm in love with you,' he forced out, pulling her against his chest and swooping down on her startled, half-open mouth with a clumsy, savage kiss that had not the remotest connection with Gail's conception of love.

A swift, brutal punishment, it was over in seconds as he pushed her roughly away. And just as quickly, out of the raw hurt he had inflicted, she gave him her answer in the livid mark staining his cheekbone scarlet.

'And that wasn't an invitation!' she cried aloud against his mockery. She waited for the sound of his laughter, his enjoyment of his cruel, cruel joke, for he would be impervious to her vicious, retaliating slap like that first time on the ferryboat. Indeed his blank, unmoving expression suggested he had scarcely noticed it. That was until he came back from his thoughts—back to her. And then Gail wanted to look away, but his eyes wouldn't let her, holding her there with their unfathomable, accusing stare. He had never been further from laughing.

'Run, and I just may drag you back by your hair.'

He read her so accurately, and his strangulated tone made her shiver. His desire to hit her was almost tangible. So why didn't he do it?—cancel out the crazy guilt that was making her think she deserved it? Soon she was shaking and, pride abandoned, she stammered, 'You . . . you're scaring me.'

'I'm *scaring* her!' Her plea for mercy brought forth laughter, harsh and joyless. 'That's rich, very rich!'

'I don't understand.' Gail knew she had somehow caused this bitterness and found herself saying in a small voice, 'I'm sorry if I hurt you.'

It did the trick, for the mercurial anger gradually dissipated, leaving him cold and unreachable. 'How could you possibly do that?'

He had taken her regret for pity, and rejected it with icy arrogance.

'I suggest we continue this discussion in my study,' he said coolly.

Gail followed him through an interconnecting door to a smaller, more private room, having observed, as he had, Joel running back to the house. He drew up a chair for her in front of a massive, leather-topped desk and moved round to the other side, removing a bottle and two glasses from a glass cabinet set against the wall.

'Drink it.'

Fragile and shaken, Gail did as he ordered, choking slightly as she drained the good measure of whisky.

He broke the mounting silence with a stiff, decisive, 'I agree that the child should have both a father and mother. The boy immediately took to you and you made your feelings patently obvious over tea. Together we could provide him with a normal home background.'

'It wouldn't work.' Gail tried so hard to sound reasonable, but it came out panicked.

His eyes narrowed, but he returned implacably, 'I don't see any insurmountable problems.'

No problems, he announced, when ten minutes in the same room had them at each other's throats! 'We dislike each other too much to . . .'

'Don't presume to know my feelings for you,' he interrupted, even while cold grey eyes told their own story. 'And I can live with your obvious dislike, provided you learn to temper it round Joel. He needs a mother, but I never wanted a permanent woman in my life to whom I would be accountable. A marriage between us is both logical and practical.'

'But what about love?' Every sensitivity cried out against his dry businesslike approach, but she cringed inwardly when she realised just what she had said.

'As you should know, marriage and love are not synonymous,' Kyle baldly cast her past up to her. 'I'm thirty-six and up till now have managed to avoid such a debilitating emotion. And you have made it crystal clear you have no desire to be . . . courted.'

The acrid stress of the old-fashioned term jarred, setting off a train of thought in Gail's head. This proposal wasn't a spur-of-the-moment idea. Kyle Saunderson didn't work like that. Mrs Macbeth's assessment of her employer came back to her—responsible and kind, especially towards life's waifs and strays. It helped form a pattern to his conflicting moods and his erratic behaviour of that afternoon, throwing them into a very different light.

'You weren't joking, were you? When you were making—' Gail shied off the word 'love', 'trying to make me like you better.' She paused, but when he was on the point of cutting in, she rushed on, 'I thought you were trying to make a fool of me, to pay me back for . . . I got it mixed up because I knew you couldn't mean it.'

'Now you've got it straight, perhaps you could let me into the secret of my motives,' he replied, not one degree warmer and with heavy irony at her near-incoherence.

'You wanted to make the idea of marriage more acceptable, but it went wrong because you and I—well, it's ridiculous, isn't it?' she appealed impulsively, and knew instantly she had put her foot in it. 'But it was very kind of you to . . .'

'I think you've made your feelings on the subject plain enough,' Kyle silenced her, before draining his glass and leaning towards her across the desk.

'Understand this, if nothing else, there was absolutely nothing kind or noble about my intentions. I'm offering you two choices. Marry me and share Joel. Or refuse, in which case I shall not allow you any contact with *my* son until he has attained his majority. He can make up his own mind if he wants to see his mother when he's old enough, but you're not going to drift in and out of our lives, reeking your own unique brand of havoc, Gail Mackenzie.'

The face lit by the flicker from his gold lighter was carved out of unyielding stone. He meant it, every hard word. Tomorrow she had intended leaving, but had she planned to stay away for ever? Gail didn't know the answer, not for sure. She hadn't seen further than getting away from Kyle Saunderson's influence.

She affected a brave, reckless air in a remark that was pure evasion. 'What are the conditions attached to this package deal, Mr Saunderson?'

For a fleeting second fury blazed at her defensive flippancy, and then he was responding in kind. 'Two conditions. You stop calling me Mr Saunderson in that prim, virginal tone.' His voice dropped lower as he pronounced with deadly seriousness, 'And that you never tell Joel that I'm not his father.'

'You can't ask that of me!' she exclaimed despairingly. There would come a time when it would have to be explained to the boy, before any mischief-maker took it upon themselves to give their version of the truth to an unsuspecting youngster. 'It's not possible!'

Crushing his cigarette out with a controlled violence, Kyle gritted contemptuously, 'Not for any silly, romantic notion does that child deserve to be told the circumstances that led to his existence.'

For once his derision didn't touch her. Making him understand was more important than anything else.

'You can't let him find out the hard way—it's just not fair! You don't know how dirty people can make you feel if you're illegitimate.' Gail stretched across the desk, grasping one of his hands to reinforce her argument. 'The snide comments from the older children, they stay with you always.'

The pressure of her fingers as much as her impassioned plea begged him to listen and heed the warning that was based on bitter, personal experience. When he loosened his hand from her compulsive grip she anticipated an outright rejection of her fears, not the warmth of his hand engulfing her much smaller one.

'Your mother must have derived great comfort from her loyal little girl.'

The purpose behind Gail's exposure of her private misery had not been to gain this soft, undermining sympathy, and extricating her fingers from his, she rebuffed his pity with complete honesty. 'My mother was bitterly ashamed of my existence till the day she died. I don't want any of that for Joel.'

'You think I do when I see what it's done to you?' he countered frustratedly. 'How many people know who was the father of the baby you bore?'

In the fading light, his head now held back in the lengthening shadows, Gail couldn't discern the direction of his thinking that led to his abrupt question. The way he referred to her baby son and the boy Joel implied that for him they were two disparate human beings.

'Three—no, two,' she assessed; Barry no longer counted. The phrase seemed strangely prophetic.

'People you trust?'

The light dawned: he thought that if they married, Joel could be passed off as their son. He was going too far and too fast for her, and she answered simply by nodding.

'I would like to forget Barry's connection with the boy. I suggest you try to do so as well. In ten years, when Joel is in adolescence and at his most vulnerable, I doubt anyone will bother relaying the fact that his parents didn't live together for the first few years of his life, and it's unlikely that he'll remember.'

Sound reasoning, but the vision of a small, bewildered boy walking in on one of their interminable squabbles made it appear more like a recipe for disaster. Fixated on that thought, Gail barely listened as Kyle outlined arrangements for a quick, discreet marriage, and when he had finished, she retreated with, 'I'd like to go upstairs and lie down for a while. I'm tired.'

He made no move to stop her, but his voice out of the near darkness reached her at the door.

'It's the right thing to do—for both of us.'

His quiet authority said the matter was settled, for better or worse, and she left him without correcting the impression.

She didn't come down to dinner but lay on top of her bedcovers, trying to persuade herself through the long evening to accept the only way by which she could have and hold her son.

She had lived with a married man and had his child out of wedlock, both of which must be damning sins, so why should she balk at this marriage? The distinction lay in the fact that she had thought she had loved Barry, but his brother she couldn't love. So why did a comparison between the two make her certain that if she had met both Saundersons on that fateful train journey, it would not have been Barry whom she would have remembered? But she had been silly and seventeen, and only a dreamer. Even if she had met the older Saunderson all those years ago, he wouldn't have spared her a second glance. So now she knew better, didn't she? She couldn't *love* him—when she shuddered every time he so much as touched her— and no doubt her granny could put a name to that treacherous feeling.

Kyle wasn't asking for her love, but was giving her the chance to fulfil a promise made to an unborn baby which in her heart she wanted to take so very badly. The doubts, however, came crowding in, and she knew it to be wrong.

CHAPTER TWELVE

'You look bloody awful, lass,' was Peter Mason's opening remark to the forlorn figure he found on his doorstep, but it was more than cancelled out by the ear-to-ear grin emerging beneath a mass of grey beard.

'And it's lovely to see you too, Peter,' Gail laughed back.

And two years dissolved in the same number of seconds, as she was whisked off her feet in a rough bear-hug that sent her cases clattering to the bottom of the steps and then given another critical inspection, before he confirmed, 'Bloody awful!'

'Flatterer!' she made a face back at him.

'Cheeky kid,' he gave back his favourite insult, and they laughed together, while Peter rescued her suitcases from the pavement.

He dumped them in the hallway of the large four-storey Georgian building, paused long enough to say, 'God, but it's good to see you, lassie,' and waved her through to the kitchen to meet the rest of the staff.

A breathless half an hour later Gail sank down on a chair in the restaurant that occupied the rest of the ground floor.

'Well, what do you think?'

'It's . . .' Gail paused, partly to once again take in the gleaming silverware, polished glass and spotless linen, but mostly to tease the man opposite her, fifty years old and eager as a schoolboy for her verdict, before pronouncing, 'Elegant.'

'Elegant—I like it.' He roared with laughter but evidently pleased by the description which was such a contrast to the man himself—a mountain of a man, looking like everybody's idea of a wild Highlander, although city born and bred and dressed in a smart lounge suit. 'And the staff?'

'They're very ... friendly,' Gail recalled an overwhelming mixture of hand-shaking and incomprehensible, but enthusiastic greetings, 'very . . .'

'Italian?' he prompted laughingly. 'Don't worry, all emotion gets expressed in their own language, but they can all speak English very well. Even Mamma Simonelli, when she wants to.'

'She's lovely.'

'She's a tyrant,' Peter declared with a groan, 'but she cooks like an angel. I hired her through an agency about a year ago, not realising that I was about to be taken over. I think we'll have to expand soon, if only to accommodate her endless supply of relatives.'

'You like her,' Gail accused, seeing through the false picture he was building round the neat, once beautiful, dark-haired woman that she had met earlier, and slanting him a purposefully knowing look, 'and you're an old fraud, if you say you don't.'

'Hey, less of the old,' he wagged a finger at her, 'and don't go typical woman on me and start matchmaking!'

'Me?' she assumed a look of total innocence that drew a smile from him.

'You, baby blue eyes.' Gail's brightness slipped for a moment, extinguished in an unpleasant echo, and Peter was quick to notice. 'What did I say?'

'Nothing,' she shook her head and continued lightly. 'Come on, I know you're dying to give me a guided tour.'

The theme of the club housed in the basement was 'turn of the century' simplicity, with natural wood contrasting the polished brass beer-pumps and the ornate gas lighting fitted in dark oak panelling. Lining the walls was a collection of sepia prints of the late Victorian London of tramcarts, and gentlemen in top hats, and ragamuffin children playing in the gutter. Peter lit the gas mantels and switched off the electric lighting, and the atmosphere was complete.

'It's . . .'

'Elegant?' Peter laughed.

'Quaint,' Gail finally decided. 'It's just perfect, and I love it.'

'She loves it,' he mimicked her forced enthusiasm, showing she wasn't fooling anybody, and throwing an arm around her shoulders, said, 'So why so tense, love?'

'I can't sing here, Peter.' Her eyes swept the tasteful décor and the superior, expensive fittings, a giant step up-market from the old club. She tried to explain, 'Folk music, it's for students with shaggy hair and wearing sloppy jerseys, not . . .'

'Civil servants and trendy lawyers and young City men,' Peter detailed his clientele, voicing her fears, then set about reducing them with, 'The same students, a few years on, wearing collar and tie but still listening to the music of their youth.'

'I don't know, Peter.'

'Well, *I* do, kiddie. OK, so we'll maybe have to update your act a bit,' he conceded, and running a critical eye over her clothing, 'And if you're a good girl, I'll buy you a dress or two.'

'Sugar-daddy!' Gail quipped.

'You should be so lucky,' Peter snorted back. 'You can pay me back out of the ridiculously generous salary I'll be paying you for airing your lungs a few hours a night.'

'I'm a damn good singer,' Gail cried indignantly.

'Who told you that?' he scoffed.

'You did.'

'Must be true, then,' he smiled back, and announced with mock seriousness, 'You're hired. Let's go and eat.'

He collected her luggage from the foyer and unlocking a

door marked 'Private' led her upstairs to his living accommodation. It was smart and functional, with strictly modern furniture of glass and steel and leather.

After lunch Peter was called away to sign for a delivery of wine, and as the minutes of his absence ticked by, Gail was left with time to think.

It had been easy to get away, simply a matter of waiting for Kyle to leave for work and Mrs Macbeth to take Joel to the nursery school he attended three mornings a week, and then walking, a bag in each hand, down to the local railway station to catch the first train to London. The tubes had been a trial, with Gail priding herself in choosing the right line and spoiling it by going east instead of west, but here she was, safe and sound—and any second, about to start crying again.

'Lass, lass, what's the matter?' Peter Mason was not particularly surprised to find a bright buoyant Gail replaced by the girl with her head in her hands, weeping her misery out. He knew both, better than most people anyway, and while the first brought out the best in him, the other made him feel murderous. 'Is it Saunderson?'

The name made Gail cry louder and he cursed himself for a rough fool, and waited until she tired herself out, holding her close and soothing with nonsense, before saying, 'Nothing's that bad, love.'

And after she had told him the full story, in fits and starts, Peter Mason wasn't so sure if he was right this time, but instead he said, 'We'll get you a lawyer—a good one.'

'A lawyer?'

'You want the boy, don't you?' Peter asked gently.

'Yes.' Gail's answer was adamant before she caught Peter's drift, and then her denial was just as forceful. 'No, Peter, not that way—I couldn't! It's not right. Kyle—he cares for him, he can protect him.'

'Listen, Gail.' Peter adopted his cruel-to-be-kind tone, 'that family forfeited any right to considerations of decency the day Barry Saunderson charmed himself into your life and then did his level best to ruin it.'

'Kyle, he's different,' she protested, too vehemently.

'How different?' Peter asked with hard suspicion.

'He's . . .' Gail searched futilely for the terms to describe him, for there were too many conflicting images. 'I don't know. Just different.'

She was having difficulty interpreting the speculative gaze Peter was training on her, but she picked upon the quiet despair in his next comment.

'Not again, Gail!'

'No!' Gail realised that she had almost shouted and instantly regretted it. She squeezed Peter's hand and smiled, 'You must think I'm soft in the head.'

'Or in the heart?' he suggested, and was rewarded with a baleful glance. 'OK, now I'm beginning to sound like a typical woman. Forget I said it.'

'And the lawyer,' Gail said anxiously.

He nodded. 'I give up on you, Gail Mackenzie.'

'That'll be the day,' she retorted.

'Cheeky kid!'

But Peter was as good as his word and never returned to the subject. For the next week he worked her hard at the new songs in the afternoons and made no comment when he found her helping out in the restaurant in the evening. She had to keep busy.

She lived in a giant, airy attic room on the top floor, for Peter, after a foray into the bedsit land of Earl's Court, had decided against her living alone, and she wasn't given the opportunity to argue. Cleared of accumulated rubbish and furnished with what Peter modestly called 'odds and ends', the room was bright and welcoming. Once Gail could have been happy there, but while the days were busy and filled with the laughing chatter of Maria Simonelli's family, the nights were long.

It was asking the impossible for her not to think of Joel,

and every time she did, she couldn't detach his image from that of Kyle, a little boy confidently hurtling into his father's outstretched arms. And sometimes it turned into the craziest of waking dreams—that it was she who was running into those strong, muscular arms, that they were closing round her and keeping her safe. It frightened her, for it came without conscious thought, and she didn't try to analyse it. It would recede in time; everything did, even pain. She had to keep telling herself that.

Long hours of practice had helped, but her first performance, plagued by nerves and under the curious scrutiny of Peter's regular clientele, was below standard. Within days, however, she was singing with the clear, sweet quality that Peter called musical magic and received an enthusiastic reception from her audience.

And things did get easier, or at least she achieved a numbness that took her through the motions. Kitted out with a wardrobe of dresses classically simple rather than glamorous and with her hair trimmed to highlight what the hairdresser had termed its 'wild natural beauty', she supposed she looked the part. Her singing Peter declared to be better than ever. In a way he was right. Nerves gone, she was slick and professional; she might be reaching her audience, but she was becoming less and less aware of them.

At the weekends Peter would accompany her on the piano, and initially she had felt naked without her guitar. But Peter, a credible entertainer in his younger days, showed her how to project the meaning of the songs with her hands and body movements and they too became part of the act.

Summer came early and the June nights were hot and sticky, even with air-conditioning. But Gail looked deliciously cool in a sleeveless bodice and lacy petticoat skirt, as she went utterly still for a moment and released the last soulful note of 'Let it be Me'. For several seconds it held her audience in absolute, spellbound silence, and when the applause broke, she swept the room encompassing the dimly-lit tables and the bar area, with a fixed detached smile.

But an overwhelming sense of *déjà-vu* froze that smile on her lips, stripping the years away till she was seventeen once more and transfixed by a hypnotic stare. Even though the moment passed under the unrelenting, ruthless gaze of the man and she was returned to the present time and place, Gail couldn't control the quivering ache that shot through her at the sight of Kyle Saunderson. It was an agonising, devastating sensation that she refused to acknowledge as anything but fright.

'Gail, for heaven's sake!'

She heard Peter's urgent whisper, knew he was repeating the opening bars of her next song, but was remote from it all, only truly conscious of the man standing at the end of the long counter, his features lit by the bar lighting.

The mocking salute as he lifted his glass to her, the triumphant curve of his mouth as he savoured the disruption his presence had caused, challenged her to run with an audience to witness her cowardice.

With imperfect timing, she joined the music, her voice barely above a whisper as she forced out familiar words that held no meaning.

'Your eyes kissed mine, I saw the love in them shine,
You brought me heaven right then when your eyes kissed mine.'

She felt *his* eyes drawing her back, compelling her not to look away and bound to him by invisible cords; again she missed the beat of the next verse, and the derisive twist of his lips betrayed his cruel enjoyment of watching her fall to pieces.

Blue eyes blazed their defiance as she waited for her cue

and then took up the refrain, only this time she did full
justice to the beautiful, traditional love song with every
clear, poignant note.

'My love loves me, and all the wonders I see,
A rainbow shines in my window, my love loves me.

And now he's gone, like a dream that fades into dawn,
But the words stay locked in my heartstrings,
"My love loves me."

The joys of love are but a moment long,
The pain of love endures the whole life long.'

If this was victory, she thought as her eyes desperately
followed his retreating back, why did it taste so sour? Kyle
had stayed to the last, lingering note, anger in every rigid
facial muscle, and then, slamming his glass hard against
the bar, had almost fled up the stairs leading to the street.
And what had happened to her fierce pride when he was
gone? The hot tears cascaded down her blanched cheeks
as she shook uncontrollably, oblivious of her stunned
audience.

It was the last time she was to sing in public. A few notes
were all she could manage before her voice broke, and all
sound dried up in her throat. No physical cause, was the
doctor's diagnosis, but after a week Gail was ready to give
up the struggle to overcome the alarming paralysis of her
vocal chords.

'You're not trying,' Peter accused, as he noisily closed
the lid of the piano and joined her at the edge of the
platform.

'I am,' Gail lied, and hugged her knees under her chin.
'It just won't come.'

'Oh, girlie!' he sighed, coming down to her level. He'd

coaxed, he'd bullied, he'd yelled, and he'd got exactly nowhere. 'You're growing apathetic, Gail.'

'No, not any more.' Kyle's appearance had destroyed that numbness inside. 'Pathetic, maybe.'

'I didn't mean it,' he denied.

'You didn't say it,' she assured him, forcing a smile.

'Oh!' He'd said so many things to try and get through to her. She was hurting, but not through him. 'Anyway, it's only been a few days since . . .'

'I made a complete idiot of myself,' Gail supplied self-mockingly.

'Is that what's bothering you?'

'No, not really.' She was being selfish, wasting Peter's time, and she concentrated her thoughts for a moment before saying slowly, 'Do you remember the first time we met—at that Gaelic concert in the island hall?'

'A little girl in a kilt down to her calves and a horrific frilly blouse,' he smiled at the memory, 'with the face and voice of an angel.'

'Charmer!' She pulled a face but reverted to seriousness with, 'On the island, singing was the most important thing in my life. I could sing better than the other girls, and that made me feel somebody—more than just the Mackenzie bastard.'

'Oh, Gail,' Peter groaned, squeezing her arm, 'nobody cares about that sort of thing any more.'

'It's okay, Peter, it's not important any more. But neither's the singing.' Gail made a helpless gesture with her hands, before continuing, 'I just can't hold on to the notes or the words in my head. They seem so trivial, meaningless when compared with . . . other things.'

'Such as?' Peter asked, even though he was pretty sure he knew the answer.

'I don't know . . . just things,' Gail muttered evasively.

'Gail, Gail, this is Peter, remember,' he scolded mildly, then with harsh, protective anger, he muttered, 'Why in heaven didn't he just leave you alone? And don't say who—Carlo, behind the bar, gave me a description of your admirer. He doesn't sound so different from the other one.'

'He is,' Gail replied succinctly, wishing Peter would leave it.

'Did you leave a forwarding address?'

She fielded his sideways glance with a resounding, 'No! Of course not.'

'So how did he find you?' Peter wondered aloud. 'London's a big place, thousands of clubs like this one.'

'He has his spies,' she attempted to joke, but it didn't come off, and she answered Peter's frown flatly, 'He probably hired a private investigator. He did the last time.'

'Heavy stuff,' Peter let out in one long breath.

'Yes, he is—heavy stuff.'

'Not so like his brother.'

Gail knew what he meant. It was true, Kyle made Barry look a lightweight. She jumped down from the platform in a quick, decisive movement.

'Where are you going?' Peter followed her down. He was worried about her and she replied, a shade too cheerfully,

'I have a date with some dishes.'

'You don't have to, you know,' he lightly reprimanded Gail's determination to pay her way. 'Maria says that soon you'll be washing them *before* she gets the food on the plate, far less to the customers.'

'Maria's a tyrant,' she laughed.

Peter clicked his tongue with mock reproof. 'You have no respect for your elders, girlie.'

'Oh, you . . . !' she cuffed him playfully and slipped her arm through his, and then, because she knew she was going to disappoint him, she said quietly, 'I may not listen, Peter, but I respect you very much. I always have.'

'Soft kid,' he muttered with pleased embarrassment, and hugged her hard for a moment. 'Come on, you wash, I'll dry.'

CHAPTER THIRTEEN

It was masochistic, maudlin and utterly foolish, but Gail knew it was worth it on her first sight of Joel, even from the hundreds of yards that separated them as she stood hidden by the trees on the far side of the lake. A second day, and then a third, as she broke the promise to herself that it would be the last day she would take the train out to the Surrey countryside. It was crazy and illogical, for hadn't she managed to survive four years without any contact? but then she hadn't known where her son was, or had a mental picture which was such a sweet torment.

Who was she harming? Only herself, she realised, as she dropped silently to the ground. She should be making plans for the future, and every day she rose with the firm intention of doing just that. And noon found her buying her ticket at Victoria, so regularly that the counter clerk had jocularly commented that morning, 'Perhaps it'd be cheaper, ducks, if you lived out there?' The black look Gail had unintentionally given him had wiped away all traces of humour.

Dressed in camouflage of green jumper and corded jeans, she cautiously hugged the thickest part of the wood, her sneakers treading soundlessly as she took a round-about route to her usual vantage point at the edge of the woodland.

The first indication that she was not alone came from the snapping of a twig, and she halted dead in her tracks. When he emerged directly on her pathway from behind a thick tree-trunk, the breath caught in her throat. Casual in denim shirt and blue jeans, she instinctively knew he had been lying in wait for her, and the smile of greeting briefly on his lips was more disconcerting than any show of dark anger.

'You're back.'

His seemingly casual acceptance of her return told her he had been expecting it and as usual had the advantage over her. She stood rigid, like a trapped animal mesmerised by the cunning of its captor.

When he would have closed the distance that lay between them, she automatically shifted backwards, and he stayed his ground.

'I knew you would be.'

It was a plain statement, with no suggestion of any knowing arrogance, as though he was treading his path with the utmost care.

'How?' she choked out.

'The irresistible attraction of one member of my household,' he declared calmly, 'but don't worry, I'm not suffering from any delusions.'

'You were waiting for me,' she said on a contradictory note of accusation. It was, after all, she who was trespassing.

'You were spotted by a friend clambering over the wall yesterday and he warned me that a red-haired thief was stalking my grounds. Today the stationmaster telephoned to tell me that you'd arrived on the one o'clock train,' he explained evenly.

'You have a lot of influence.' Gail was genuinely amazed at how easily Kyle remained a jump ahead all the time, or so it seemed.

'You'd better start believing it.'

The cool words held a threat, although his mouth formed a conciliatory smile. Hands resting on narrow hips and feet set apart, ready for the possibility of chase, he looked more than capable of dealing with one small, insignificant girl.

'I do.'

'Joel's missed you.' The widening of sapphire blue eyes registered disbelief. 'The mother-and-child bond isn't one-way, you know.'

'I didn't want to go.'

'I know,' he responded gravely to her appeal for understanding. Shoving his hands into his back pockets, for once he seemed less than certain of every move as he turned his head momentarily to the house and then back to face her. 'This is ridiculous.'

'Yes,' she agreed huskily, simultaneously aware of the absurdity of a conversation conducted over a distance of twenty yards.

'Come up to the house, Gail.'

Order or request, her delay was momentary.

And so it was that she drifted back into the life at Barlington Hall. Once at the house, Kyle disappeared, leaving Mrs Macbeth to rustle up a late lunch for their 'guest', and afterwards, when Joel eagerly followed his instructions to take Gail on a tour of the stables at the rear and proudly showed her his own pony, a shaggy, placid Shetland comically misnamed Flash, Kyle effectively preempted any attempt on her part to drift out.

Returning via a wide sweep of the lake suggested by Joel, delighted that everyone seemed to have forgotten his afternoon nap, Gail was confronted in the chequered hallway by her luggage. And while she obeyed Kyle's impassive instruction to follow him, Joel kept up his excited chatter all the way to a room at the end of the upper gallery and rendered any discussion between the adults virtually impossible. Laying her cases on the bed, Kyle said quietly, 'Mason sent them,' before leaving her alone with Joel, who had piped up with an offer to help her with her unpacking. Gail concentrated all her attention on the small, red-headed boy who was making short work of her task by heaping most of her clothes in the bottom drawer of the tallboy.

Through the long English summer they lived in harmony, or as near that state as their tacit agreement to avoid conflict allowed. There were dangerous moments when they were one short step away from explosion, and Gail accepted that they were created by her, and averted by Kyle's superb self-control that left her ashamed of her immaturity.

But mostly their time alone, during dinner, was passed on a polite, impersonal level to which they both rigidly adhered.

Their meeting ground was Joel, in whose presence they laid aside any enmity, and gradually each came to abandon that guarded wariness of the other, to the extent that Gail would find herself laughing naturally at his dry, witty remarks and responding in kind. That was, until she caught one of his watchful, appraising looks on her flushed, happy face, and sobered almost instantly.

To the outside world, however, they must have appeared as the perfect family unit of strict but tolerant father, devoted mother and much loved child, and it was inevitable that mistakes should be made concerning her relationship to Kyle. Yet each time she was referred to as his wife by strangers, she was unable to prevent a telltale blush staining her dimpled cheeks. She would look down at her feet, or move away from his side to divorce herself from the incident, or suddenly scoop up Joel, who was always ready to be cuddled—anything to avoid that cynical twist of his mouth she had witnessed the first time the assumption had been made.

Worse were Mrs Macbeth's not-so-subtle attempts at matchmaking; no matter how loudly Gail made discouraging noises, the Scottish nanny was determined to see a happy ending to the uneasy alliance. Second sight, Mrs Macbeth called it; Gail thought it more the result of double vision. That Kyle had not the remotest intention of repeating his cold-blooded offer of marriage became increasingly obvious with the passing of the months, and his avoidance of discussing the future, her future over which he had such an alarming power, alternately scared and angered her. Scared, she tried to melt into the background of his life; angered, in a mood of confused self-destruction, she demanded to know how long he would allow her to remain, and was overwhelmed with relief when he looked straight through her, before walking away leaving her question hanging.

Each day made it more difficult to imagine life without the lively four-year-old who needed no excuse to smile at the world and to Gail, rarely showed any of his stubborn streak, but unquestioningly returned her love; or without Simon, home for the holidays and proving that beneath his tendency to adopt a solemn attitude to life there lay a bright, intelligent personality. After an initial mutual guardedness, they accepted each other and graduated to an easy, natural friendship. With the engaging self-importance of a boy used to taking rather than giving instructions to an adult, he taught her how to fish and canoe. And Gail, in turn, gave him music lessons on the guitar.

Sometimes she surprised herself by wishing she was one of the children who received Kyle's caring attention. Not that he was unpleasant to her; he treated her with a faultless courtesy that was remote and unchallenging. She should have been grateful—instead she found herself struggling against a crazy urge to shout at him, 'Stop looking straight through me! See me. I'm a person. I'm a woman and I want . . .' What did she want? Anything other than that distant front he presented that at times seemed worse than any cruelty or sarcasm.

Gail scanned the contents of her wardrobe for the third time and gave up in despair. There were the dresses she'd bought in London, but, despite their undoubted prettiness, they were not what she wanted for tonight. Kyle had announced at breakfast that he was entertaining some friends to dinner and expected her to attend. Forestalling her certain objection, he had drained his coffee cup and strode out of the dining room. It was to Mrs Macbeth, in charge of the arrangements, Gail went to discover who would be at this dinner. Ten people including Kyle and herself, and only two of the rest she had actually met—Dr Tanner, who had attended her during her illness, and Laura Petrie.

Thoughts of the always elegant, poised Miss Petrie had sent her flurrying up to her room to find something suitable to wear at the dinner party, the first Kyle had given since her arrival. Again, Gail flicked through her collection of dresses. Most of them looked fresh and new, so why were they suddenly unsuitable? It wasn't a beauty competition she was entering.

Hours later she stared disbelievingly into the full-length mirror, disconcerted rather than pleased with the image reflected by the glass. It had taken a frustratingly long time to do anything about her hair, but now it was arranged on the top of her oval-shaped head in a style that would have been a credit to any professional hairdresser. The blue silk of the dress she had eventually purchased after an exhausting round of the better off-the-peg London fashion shops clung to every curve of her no longer emaciated body. The high mandarin collar at the neckline and the long, straight sleeves contrasted in their demureness with the slits at the sides of the Chinese-patterned gown, designed to allow freedom of movement.

'You *have* style,' she tried to convince the girl in the glass, but an inner voice mocked her efforts with a smart 'Who are you trying to fool?' Nobody. She wasn't trying to fool anybody—she just wanted to hold her own with

Laura Petrie, who contrived to make her feel gauche and young in front of Kyle.

It took courage, born of pride, to keep descending the wide sweep of stairs under that penetrating, disapproving stare. By the time Gail reached their foot, defiance warred with an unaccountable hurting. So he didn't like it. What did it matter to her? The frank, warm appreciation in Dr Tanner's eyes was confirmation that she looked good. Tilting her head higher, she bestowed a dazzling smile on Kyle before extending a hand to the young doctor, who was extremely gallant in his remarks on his former patient's appearance.

It set the mood for the evening. The more Kyle glared at her across the length of the oak table, the more she sparkled for the young man seated on her left and the more mature, but nonetheless admiring, Colonel Spencer Petrie, Laura's father. With none of his daughter's pretension, his conversation amused and relaxed, his courtly attention contrasted sharply with the displeasure emanating from Kyle Saunderson whenever Gail caught his cold eyes on her—inevitable as they sat directly opposite each other. Totally bewildered by it, she wanted to cry out that he didn't have to watch her as though she was in danger of using the wrong fork or liable to say anything indiscreet. Instead she behaved impeccably.

By the end of the evening she had charmed the men and made friends of the women, except for Laura, who had rarely left Kyle's side, intent on monopolising his attention. When Gail stood on the threshold of the front door, her farewells were warm and natural, and Spencer Petrie's conspiratorial whisper that she could climb over *his* boundary wall any time she had a mind to added to the feeling that the evening had been a successful one.

But the moment the double-fronted doors closed on the

last guest, she made for the stairs, only to be halted by an angry-voiced Kyle.

'Wait!'

She didn't turn, but said as composedly as she could manage, now they were alone and the sound of his short, sharp command echoed through the emptiness of the large hall, 'I'm tired. I want to go to bed.'

'And I want to talk to you,' he responded in a tone that indicated that his desires overrode her inclinations.

Gail spun round to face him and with anger uppermost, said tautly, 'Despite your frosty glares, I've enjoyed this evening, and I'm not letting you spoil it for me.'

Every step up the long staircase she sensed his eyes boring into her back, but she kept it rigid, her carriage stiffly upright. At the top, she made for the nursery as she always did last thing, to watch Joel sleeping by his nightlight. Even in the short time she had been here, he had grown; it reminded her of how much she had already missed of his development.

Five minutes later she was already regretting her rash refusal to talk with Kyle. Perhaps she'd better go down and say . . . what? That she was sorry, when she had no real inkling what had caused his foul mood? Maybe it wasn't with her, she mused hopefully, and instantly dismissed it as wishful thinking; she had seen him too often with Laura Petrie not to know that *she* never annoyed him. One foot on the first step Gail changed her mind. Tomorrow—she'd see him tomorrow and pray by that time he would have forgotten this disastrous evening which she had made a pretence of enjoying from that first cold, disapproving stare.

She crossed her bedroom by moonlight, undoing the diagonal row of pearl buttons across the neckline of her dress. She fumbled for the bedside lamp, and recoiled from the sight revealed by its muted glare.

'Get out!' The order was instinctive. The menace lay

not in his apparent body lounging in the armchair at the far side of the bed—legs stretched out in front—but in the grey eyes, insolent and stripping, as they travelled over the curves outlined in perfect detail by the Chinese silk.

'I shouldn't bother,' he mocked her attempt to refasten the open buttons. 'I can use my imagination, like any other man.'

He made a move to rise and she panicked. But before she could reach the corridor, she was slammed against the door, cornered by two arms pinning her body to the wooden panelling. After all these months of Kyle's politeness, she had been unprepared for (had tried to erase) the almost barbaric side of his nature. She couldn't suppress the tremor running through her slight frame; he was frightening her—and badly.

'I . . . I don't understand,' she stuttered. As an answer he came closer still, until the silk of her dress seemed to be all that separated them. 'Please, Kyle.'

His words were a low, vicious growl in his throat. 'You've got them all, haven't you? Your cousin, Mason . . . even Tanner. And you pretend you don't understand!'

'I don't.' Her plea was barely above a whisper. Let him explain what she had done that was so wrong—or give her a chance.

'How does it feel? To be so powerful?' His hand gripped her chin, forcing her head upwards. 'Yo have them all worshipping at your altar?'

'You're mad!' she exclaimed. 'Rory is my cousin—and you know I made those things up about him.'

'Do I? Perhaps I was mad—mad enough to have wanted to give you my protection,' he muttered raggedly. His fingers slid round the soft curve of her neck. 'But you can do that to men, can't you?'

'I never asked you for anything,' Gail protested vehemently.

'No, that's your style, Gail Mackenzie—you don't ask,

you never ask,' he rasped, increasing the pressure at her neck until she felt he might be about to break it. 'You'll leave another of your farewell notes, terse to the point of rudeness, but you'll still have me following you—even when I know you have a new "protector"!'

The slur of his last words gave a wealth of meaning that made them an insult. At last, Gail saw what he was doing; he was trying to put their relationship back to its original footing by rekindling the rage that used to spark between them. And herself? She realised she had been a fool to hope that the times they had spent together, both with and without the children, had been the beginnings of something else . . .

'Please, Kyle,' she entreated, clutching at his shoulders, 'there was nothing between myself and Peter Mason either. He was my employer and friend.' If anything his expression darkened further at the word 'friend' and she rushed on, 'He's fifty years old. He treats me like a kid.'

'Your *old* friend felt young and fit enough to want to fight me over your things, and even after I got through to him you were back voluntarily, he issued some threats, more sophisticated but on the same lines as your cousin's.'

Gail had been back to see Peter, but the subject of the Saundersons had become taboo. She could well imagine, however, his reaction.

'But I suppose you have a perfectly innocent explanation for that as well,' he sneered.

He doesn't want to listen, Gail thought, but she had to make him. She suppressed her panic—fearing that this was the prelude to him asking her to go—and tried to sound calm and reasonable. 'I met Peter on the island and because he asked me to come and sing in his club in Edinburgh, he misguidedly feels responsible for the trouble I got myself into. He didn't think Barry was right for me, but I didn't heed his warnings. And I guess he was hostile to you because he sees the resemblance between you and him,' she deduced nervously.

'Are we so alike—my brother and I?' asked Kyle, shifting his grip to her upper arms when she tried to edge away.

Gail was not deceived by the quietened tone; somehow she had succeeded in moving them to more treacherous ground. If she had known the answer he wanted to hear, she would have given it to him, but she didn't. Mute and despairing, she looked away from his taut, unyielding expression.

'No,' he muttered savagely, 'not to you. Not even when you shut your eyes and try to pretend. Barry took and abused you, and left the mark of his possession like a brand.'

Her cry was anguished. 'And you won't let me forget, will you?' One mistake for which she had paid and was still paying. 'Barry's dead, damn you!' Dead and gone, and she wanted to be free of him.

'But his ghost lives on.' His laugh was short and bitter. 'Conjured up by the sweet magic of a siren. "But the words stay locked in my heartstrings, my love loves me",' he quoted the words of the song he had disrupted with his appearance at the club, but he stripped them of any tender emotion. 'He's here in the room with us, Gail, isn't he?'

'Yes!' she threw back at him with a fierceness that was all hurt. The memory of Barry was there, but only because he kept putting it there to drive a wedge in the tenuous state of peace between them. Gail cursed herself for the vain hopes she had allowed herself to cherish. 'Yes, he'll always be here with us,' she cried desperately, renewing her futile struggle to be out of Kyle's arms, and when she went still again, she could almost touch the anger within him.

'Your foolish heart may be buried with my noble brother, but I hold your beautiful body,' he murmured throatily, while his eyes roamed over the white skin bared by the opening of her dress. His fingers trailed slowly over the swell of her breast under its silk covering down to her waist and spread over her stomach in a movement that sent a shudder through her frame.

'And it's for *me*, you tremble like a virgin who has never known a man.'

The instant his voice and touch changed to that of a lover, her body began to be excited by the feel of his sure, arousing hands, to betray her, as did her entreaty of, 'Don't do this to me, Kyle!' Make her feel, make her want him—and leave her wide open to all the pain that she knew would follow.

'But you've got me too,' he ground out, forcing her against him to become aware of his needs, his desire for her.

'I didn't . . .' He placed a finger to her lips, tracing their outline and robbing her of the breath to utter a denial that did not ring true. Was that what she had been doing? Demanding this recognition of her as a woman, given by every hard muscle pressing her back against the door? Only she was losing her self in the process, as her own clamouring senses began to take over from reason.

Slowly, as though he had her consent for the action, Kyle pulled the few remaining pins from her hair and tumbled it down about her shoulders, his eyes never leaving her face—hypnotic eyes that kept her still in his arms. And then he stood back from her, and she knew he was giving her the chance to run away again—to seek the safety of the nursery. She should run, but she was caught in a trap of her own making, with her heart no longer listening to the rulings of her head. 'Couldn't love him,' she now realised, had always meant 'shouldn't love him'—but either way it made no difference now.

Done with waiting, Kyle reached out for her in the half-light and her lips whimpered their last, dying protest against the mouth that descended to claim her surrender. And then his hands were caressing, gentle and lingering on the soft, burning flesh. His fingers were gradually exposing, meeting no resistance when they eventually slid her silk to the floor, and she broke the silence with a moan of sweet, agonised longing at the tantalising play of his fingertips on her already hardened nipples.

A confusion of shame and desire had her burying her head against his shoulders, but he moved away from her, gripping her shaking fingers and placing them on the open neck of his shirt front. 'Touch me, Gail,' he ordered thickly. And no more words were spoken.

He led her nearer the weak rays of the light and his eyes, glazed with passion, were saying he found her nakedness beautiful. And Gail, all shyness gone from her, returned his steady gaze with wonder.

It seemed right to go voluntarily into his arms, and the sensation of him brushing against her had the power to make her forget all that had gone before: so that there existed the present and her overwhelming, doomed love for the man she had fought so long against loving. He cradled her head and she circled his waist with her arms, and they stood motionless for endless moments, each savouring the touch of the other, until Gail moved her mouth against the roughened skin of his muscular chest.

The moist trailing of her lips caused an explosion that broke the tender restraint in him as he crushed her down on the bed. Yet for all his urgency, he took time to pleasure her, to make her ready for his complete possession, until she was unconsciously moaning his name. And she was with him every step of the steady, rhythmic climb to a height that made her dizzy with its devastating elation . . .

But she couldn't stay at the summit for ever, free and mindless and soaring. And when they descended, the sound of their breathing vibrating the tense air, they were no longer together, and Gail cried silent tears for the loss, as Kyle lay beside her, not touching, receding further from her with each passing second. When he turned towards her, she hid her face in the pillow.

'Forgive me,' he whispered, as a tentative hand reached her shoulder.

Was he already regretting their lovemaking? Gail couldn't bear to listen to him destroying the beauty of that moment. Before she could reach the floor, his hand snaked out, catching her wrist and jerking her back to the centre of the double bed.

'Where do you think you're going?' he demanded brokenly, no vestige of the lover remaining in the grim, angular features.

She told the truth. 'I don't know—anywhere,' she cried out. 'You had to have everything, didn't you? Well, now you've got it. There isn't any more.' Pride made her voice hard and uncaring, for she had truly given him everything, only he had no use for even her gift of love.

Kyle wrenched her face round with the flat of his hand so she had no choice but to suffer his penetrating look. Gail imagined him capable of discerning the love clutching at her heart, meeting it with scorn, or worse, pity, and she shuttered her emotions from him.

'You still don't know, do you?' His eyes raked her facial expression.

'Don't know what? That you despise me.' Her tone was strident with hurt and defensiveness, in her determination to salvage her pride. 'Don't worry—I don't suffer from delusions either. Lust from any angle is unmistakable. I doubt even if it was me you wanted, but the common tart you see me as. Well, I'm sorry if I've disappointed you with my lack of experience, but I've known no other man than your brother. Try me again in a few years. Maybe by that time I shall have learned a few tricks of the trade!'

'Shut up!' he shouted, rolling the weight of his body against her once more. '*I* don't want to hear it!'

But Gail couldn't stop, all the mounting hurt of years spilling out in one angry torrent. 'You don't want to hear it! Damn you to hell, Kyle Saunderson! You want me to curl into a corner and die of shame because I once dared to think myself in love with one of your lofty family and to show that love in a way that seemed to be right. So you've made me see that what Barry and I had was unreal, transitory, built on our mutual weaknesses, but you're not going to make me bow my head for the rest of my life because of it!'

He had allowed her to continue, but the flow of words dried up at the sudden softening of his eyes and mouth, and the traitorous stirrings of her awakening body trapped against his. What had she said to cause the harshness to disappear?

'You really believe all that junk?—that I don't like the idea of Barry and yourself because of some idiotic snobbishness?' He moved back from her, then pulled her round so that they lay on their sides facing each other, and she quivered as he drew his palm from shoulder to rounded hip. 'At least our bodies have no difficulty in communicating.'

'Are you trying to tell me I *imagined* you hated the idea?' she protested, desperately clinging on to the anger while her failing instinct urged her to go into his arms and be thankful for what little he might be willing to give her.

'Oh, I hate it all right,' he admitted quietly, 'but the only snob around here is you, Gail Mackenzie. Even your nose tilts naturally in the air!'

He accompanied the teasing comment with the trail of one finger down her small, pert nose.

'Then why?' Gail urged.

Ignoring her question, he stroked the hair back from her face and traced the outline of her features with apparent satisfaction, before breathing lowly, 'Why did you let me love you?'

His steady, unwavering gaze was compelling her to be honest with herself as well as him. 'I wanted you to.'

'Sometimes, Gail Mackenzie, you can be so shockingly forthright,' he laughed, and this time the laughter reached his eyes. 'I guess that reckless courage was the first thing that had me falling in love with you, or perhaps it was the sight of bright red-gold hair tousling round your agonisingly lovely face.'

What cruel game was he playing now? 'You can't love me,' she echoed the thoughts of cold reasoning, furious and hurting that he would take her for a gullible fool with his sugar-coated lies. 'You can't love me! I'm nobody, and an expensive dress isn't going to alter the fact that inside I'm naïve and gauche and ordinary.' She stiffened in the arms that had gone out to her and rejected his false declaration with a fiery, 'Keep your pretty speeches for Laura Petrie! She has your necessary qualities of style and breeding.'

'You're not jealous, are you?' Kyle challenged softly, his mouth moving against her ear and nipping the lobe to evoke a response.

'No!' she protested adamantly, but her attempts to push him away were becoming half-hearted, to say the least. 'You give her nothing I would want!'

'How unusually perceptive of you—and to think of my nearly wasted effort in that direction!' he groaned aloud. He brushed the skin of her neck with his lips before continuing, 'Still, I don't think I'll have to fend off any more amorous advances from that predatory lady. She couldn't fail to notice that the debonair, sophisticated Kyle Saunderson was in grave danger of making a complete ass of himself by punching one or two of his male guests on the nose for just looking at you in a certain way!'

The world had gone mad, or perhaps it was just she that was losing her grip on reality, dreaming while she was awake that Kyle was speaking of love in that soft, undermining tone, while his hands slipped beneath the cover he had slipped over them, to stroke her quivering, responsive flesh.

'You don't have to pretend. Even *I* know that a man can make love to a woman without any love or liking at all. You wanted me and I, admit it, wanted you. But now it's over.' Gail gasped as his fingers dug into her waist.

'It's not over,' he denied, his lips persuasive on her sensitive throat. 'I could pleasure you again, make my name a sweet, hungry moan on your lips.'

At last she managed to twist out of his arms, clutching the sheet with a belated modesty, before she rounded on him with, 'You're the most conceited brute I've ever met!'

'Stop it, Gail, you don't need that fierce pride—not as a weapon against me, anyway.'

Tenderly he framed her face with his large hands. 'Listen to me, darling girl, and try to understand.' He hesitated, no trace of the confident aristocrat left as his voice vibrated with his own bad memories. 'My father— he was a proud, stubborn man and he frightened my mother into leaving him. He couldn't forgive her for it, nor for dying before he could swallow that pride enough to ask her to come back to us. He spent the rest of his meaningless life cursing her and every woman he used and discarded in an attempt to forget the love he saw as weakness. His unrelenting bitterness made Barry insecure and me selfish and cynical, determined to avoid any emotion that caused my father such grief.' He paused for her to absorb this information, and continued jerkily, 'I wasn't ready for you. Do you see that?'

'You called me a whore.' Gail flayed herself with the remembered abuse while all the softness in her wanted to believe.

'Please Gail, have pity on me,' Kyle whispered tormentedly. 'You were my brother's mistress. Before he died he talked incessantly about you. But there was no

vestige of any sweet vulnerability in the girl I first met—
and I thought him a fool. Only within hours I began to
realise the joke was on me. I tortured myself with the
vision of you with other men in a futile effort to kill any
good feeling towards you.'

'There was just Barry. Please believe me, Kyle.'

'Oh, Gail, I think I've known that since our first kiss on
the ferryboat,' he immediately responded to her anxious
entreaty. 'But in a way that made it worse. I set out to
taint your memories of Barry, and in the end I was willing
to offer myself as a substitute. When you returned from
London, I thought I could wait—but you played havoc
with my plans when you walked down the stairs tonight,
looking so breathtaking and defying me with a smile of
pure impudence. You were right—I wanted everything,
but now I'm asking you for anything you're prepared to
give—just don't run away again.'

His love was in the lightening of his intense, pain-filled
eyes as he gazed at her face, and she understood the agony
and jealousy that had lain behind the displays of anger
and contempt with which he had sought to wound her.
She still didn't know why, but he loved her.

His long fingers spread on her cheekbones and became
wet with the tears trickling from her wondering eyes. 'You
have everything. More than I have given of myself to
anyone.' Her tone was at odds with a confession of love,
but she saw he understood. Her misery was sharp in the
face of the impossibility of a happy ending. 'But it
wouldn't work. You'll never be able to forget Barry and
you'd end up hating me,' she sobbed her fears aloud.

Kyle's reply was measured, and he stated with a return
of his overwhelming self-confidence, 'Barry was many
things—weak, charming, irresponsible, amusing—and he
was my brother and I loved him. And then I met you and
for a while I thought I'd hate him for the rest of my life
because he knew you first when you were that happy

laughing girl in his photographs—fresh and open and unspoiled. But he's dead. And I'm alive and I hope I'll have you for ever. To be the one who receives all that fierce, loyal loving. In my eyes you're still the same girl and I want to make you happy and bring back the laughter.' He forestalled her protest by placing his finger-tips on her lips. 'Don't worry, my love isn't blind. You are also tempestuous, wilful, proud.'

'And you're . . .'

By the time he lifted his mouth from hers, Gail had forgotten the words of her counter-attack and her eyes roamed his face, no longer hiding anything. 'I love you, Kyle Saunderson, but it hurts.'

'Yes, I know. Perhaps that's what meant by the pain of loving—the wanting, the aching, the doubting. But we'll re-write that song you persecuted me with, and make the joy of love last our whole life long,' he promised. Thread-ing his fingers through her hair, he gently teased her mouth with his. 'Just as soon as you ask me.'

'Ask you?' Gail quizzed the sudden amusement pulling at the corners of his mouth.

'Well, my ego couldn't stand another refusal,' he drawled, 'and I believe it's your turn, if this is to be an equal partnership.'

She felt the beginnings of the joy he was so sure about, and smiled up at him, giving her trust. 'Kyle, will you marry me? Please?'

'Mm, I'll think about it,' he said with mock seriousness, and then knocked the affronted breath from her by hold-ing her so close it hurt. But the fighting was over, the loving begun, and she had her answer.